THOMAS ANGEL

AND THE ORDER OF THE

CATAIBH

V.S. MINOU

SilverWood

Published in 2019 by SilverWood Books

SilverWood Books Ltd
14 Small Street, Bristol, BS1 1DE, United Kingdom
www.silverwoodbooks.co.uk

ISBN 978-1-78132-901-6 (paperback)
ISBN 978-1-78132-902-3 (ebook)

British Library Cataloguing in Publication Data
A CIP catalogue record for this book is
available from the British Library

Page design and typesetting by SilverWood Books
Printed on responsibly sourced paper

For Willow, whose love and loss inspired this book

THOMAS ANGEL AND THE ORDER OF THE CATAIBH

To Bonnie

Always remember the power
is within you —

Love

Vivienne xxx

Prologue

'He lives.'

The words were barely audible as Kasperi whispered them to Sophia. She lifted his gnarled paw to her lips and kissed it gently, her whiskers tickling his claws as she did so.

'I did it for you, Sophia.'

'Kasperi, don't leave me.'

He lightly squeezed her paw, then left this life and moved into the next realm.

Far away in Edinburgh, little did Thomas Angel know that with those words his life, and the lives of those he loved, would change forever.

ONE

Edinburgh, 1890

Tom Angel walked out of the dark orphanage into the bright crispness of a September morning. As he stood there breathing in the chilly air, the thick wooden door slammed shut behind him. Spinning round at the sound, the words, Edinburgh Orphans' Hospital, carved above the door frame, caught his eye. He swallowed down a mewl that was forming in his throat.

The city lay before his paws, full of adventure and fun. However Tom, being Tom, could only see a future filled with fear and uncertainty. With one last glance back at the place that had been his home his whole life, he picked up the small battered case containing his few possessions and started off down the path.

Tom had only walked as far as Belford Bridge before

he stopped. Leaning over and looking at the water roaring past below, he could see fish jumping through the spray.

'Don't do it! Tom! Get away from the edge!'

Tom looked up. He recognised the voice, but it couldn't be, could it? Without warning, he was knocked off his paws by a black furry dervish. The pair of them fell over Tom's case and landed in a heap on the pavement. Staring into his face was Zachariah Black, a previous inmate of the orphanage, and his best friend.

'Hello,' said Zachariah, trying to untangle himself from Tom, and grinning. 'Sorry about that. I thought you were going to go over the edge there.' He nodded towards the bridge. 'Sorry.'

Zachariah pulled Tom to his chest and hugged him tightly. Tom hadn't seen his friend since he left the orphanage six months before, but Zachariah had now transformed into a gentlecat. His fur was glossy black, his clothes well cut and tailored. He looked like a dandy.

'You look, well, amazing, Zachariah! How are you?' Tom smiled, shocked and delighted at the appearance of his friend.

'Never mind me. How are you? I went looking for you at the orphanage, but they said you had already left. Where are you headed to?'

Tom shrugged his shoulders, too embarrassed to

say he was headed for Holyrood Park, where the waifs and strays of the city lived.

'Well then,' Zachariah said, brushing off Tom's embarrassed shrug, 'you're coming to stay with me. I'm living with my Aunt Claudia. She's not a bad old cat and leaves me the run of the house.'

Tom reddened. He was only too aware how he looked in his shabby worsted wool jacket and frayed trousers. Zachariah was a different cat now; he couldn't possibly want to be friends with Tom.

'That's very kind of you, but I couldn't possibly impose on you and your aunt,' he mumbled instead.

Zachariah waved away the suggestion with a well-manicured paw. 'Tom, you always looked out for me in the orphanage. Now it's my turn to repay some of that kindness you showed to a small, unwanted, black kitten a long time ago.'

Tears swelled in Tom's eyes and Zachariah looked away whilst he composed himself.

'As long as you're sure it wouldn't be any trouble to you or your aunt.'

'It would be doing me a favour. A friend to hang out with is just what I need, and Claudia thinks you will keep me on the straight and narrow.' He winked and touched the side of his nose with his paw.

Zachariah had always been a charmer with the

queens, and Tom could see by the admiring glances he was receiving from those who were passing by that nothing had changed.

He had often wondered how on earth he and Zachariah were friends. In comparison to the self-assured, funny, beautiful cat that Zachariah was, Tom was shy, scrawny, soft-hearted and ginger. A tenderpaw, as someone once told him. He had often wished he had some of Zachariah's poise, but that just wasn't Tom.

Tom picked up his case, holding it by the piece of string that served as its handle. Zachariah linked his arm though Tom's, and they started off for his aunt's house, chatting on the way.

'So, how's it been since I left, Tom?' Zachariah asked, blowing on his paw to warm it.

Tom's shoulders fell.

'Well, it's been fine, really. The other kittens left me alone. I just kept to myself, you know.' He looked at Zachariah. 'I missed you. Anyway, enough about me. What have you been up to?' Tom hoped to divert attention away from his bleak existence and back to his friend.

'Claudia had been living in the Far East for years and only found out about my parents dying and me being placed in the Orphans' Hospital when she came back. By then I had left, and when she found me, I was living on the streets. She took me in, cared for me, and when I told her about you, well, she told me to come and get you out of there.' Zachariah stopped walking and looked at Tom. 'I couldn't imagine you on the streets, Tom. You're too soft-hearted to survive. So, when I came back to find you, and they said you had already left, I thought I had lost you forever. But then I found you!'

Tom beamed back at Zachariah. He was the closest thing to family Tom had. Zachariah had come to the orphanage a few weeks after Tom, and they were placed in the same sleeping basket. When Zachariah had come of age, he had to leave the orphanage. Now Tom was the same age, it was his turn to leave the only home he ever knew.

They turned up their collars and kept their paws in their pockets as they walked at a good pace away from their past. Before long, Zachariah stopped in front of a Georgian townhouse and started searching through his pockets for a key. Before he could find one, the door was opened from the inside by a maid who curtseyed and stepped aside to allow their entry.

'Morning, Agatha,' Zachariah said. 'Is Claudia up yet?'

'Yes, sir,' she replied, curtseying again. 'She's in the dining room.'

'Good. This is Tom, by the way. He'll be staying with us. Please take his belongings up to our rooms.'

The maid eyed the suitcase suspiciously before taking it by the string handle and, with a final curtsey, disappeared up a staircase.

They entered the hallway. It was airy and light; a large window on the corner of the stairs dappled the flagstones with the light that shone through. A voice called out from one of the rooms.

'Zachariah, is that you?'

'Yes, Claudia, and I found the friend I was telling you about.' Zachariah led the way into a room to the left of the hallway. 'This, Aunt Claudia, is Tom Angel.'

They entered a warm and bright room. An elegant silver tabby was seated at the head of a long, polished, wooden dining table. She wore a full-length, corseted dress of turquoise blue, with a matching morning jacket. Her jewellery was expensive but discreet. She stood up and held out a petite, delicate paw to Tom.

'Tom, I'm so glad that Zachariah found you. He was quite adamant that he wanted to bring you here to stay with us. I do hope you will stay. You will, won't you?' She looked from Zachariah to Tom. Zachariah was looking at the carpet. He had had the good grace to blush.

'Come now, both of you sit. Look at you, Tom, you must be starving.' Claudia rang a small bell beside her, and Agatha appeared from the hallway.

They ate a hearty breakfast of poached chicken and scrambled eggs, with the creamiest milk Tom had ever tasted. Claudia chatted with him, keeping the tone light and amiable. When she had finished, Claudia excused herself saying she had work to do and left the room, leaving them to carry on eating.

'I'll help you clear the dishes and then I'll go out and find a job,' said Tom, scooping another spoonful of scrambled eggs into his mouth.

'Nonsense. We've got a lot of catching up to do. You need some new clothes, and then we'll worry about the future. You forget, I know what it felt like in the orphanage – always looking over your shoulder, always trying to protect yourself and your belongings from other cats. Well, you can forget that world, Tom. You're here now, safe, and for long as you want.'

Zachariah placed his fork on his empty plate and stretched. 'Now, enough talk. I feel like I need to work that breakfast off a bit.' He rubbed his stomach appreciatively. 'Let's get some fresh air and make you look more like the gentlecat you truly are.' Zachariah threw his napkin onto the table and pushed his chair back. He rang a little bell that sat on the table and within seconds Agatha appeared.

'Agatha, please tell Claudia that we've gone out, but we will see her for dinner.'

Agatha performed a little curtsey and left the room.

'What about the dishes?' asked Tom. He was used to doing chores in the orphanage.

Zachariah shook his head. 'That's Agatha's job, Tom, not yours. Come on, let's go.'

Picking up their jackets, they left the house and started the steep walk up to Queen Street. By the time they reached the crest of the hill, Tom was out of breath and sweating.

'Not the fittest cat in Edinburgh, are you, Tom!' Zachariah laughed. He looked as though he had strolled through the gardens on a spring morning. 'Catch your breath for a moment. We're nearly there.'

Tom leaned on the stone wall encircling the gardens and rubbed at the stitch in his side. Taking his handkerchief from his pocket, he mopped his face and whiskers.

'I'm fine now. If I hadn't have eaten so much at breakfast I would have been fine, really,' he said, between deep breaths.

Zachariah laughed and put his paw on Tom's shoulder. 'Whatever you say. Shift your bahookie then. Let's go.'

They crossed the road and stopped at the imposing door of O'Neill's Purveyors of Fine Felinewear. Zachariah rang the doorbell and waited.

The door was opened by a young cat, well dressed and groomed to perfection.

'Mr Black,' he said, 'good to see you again. Please let me take your hat and cane – and follow me.'

They were ushered into a spacious hallway that led straight into what looked like a gentlecats' club. Leather armchairs were spaced throughout the room with small tables between them, and the smell of old leather and beeswax permeated the place. Around the walls were glass cases with all manner of clothing – in one there was the most beautifully cut suiting, in another the finest cashmere scarves and gloves. The place was as quiet as a library, even though they were not the only cats there.

Zachariah nodded to an elderly cat as the assistant lead them to two seats and asked if they would like refreshments. Zachariah declined, and they both sat. Almost immediately another cat, with fur that gleamed like gold, appeared and addressed Zachariah.

'Mr Black, how wonderful to see you again. How may I be of assistance to you today?'

'My friend here is in need of some of your excellent suits,' Zachariah said, gesturing towards Tom who was trying his best to disappear into the chair he was sitting in. The colour rose in Tom's cheeks. There was no way on earth he could afford anything from a place like this.

'Of course, Mr Black,' the assistant said, and turned to Tom.

'Sir, if you would be so good as to accompany me.' He gestured for Tom to follow and walked towards a large fitting room.

Tom started to protest to Zachariah, but he ushered him away with a shake of his paw. Reluctantly, Tom followed the assistant, his cheeks still burning with embarrassment.

Once in the fitting room, the assistant asked Tom to remove his jacket and trousers, the regulation ones given to every male cat when leaving the orphanage, then stood in front of him, appraising. Fighting the urge to wrap himself in his arms, Tom wished the ground would open up and swallow him, and his shabby orphanage-issue clothing, all up.

'Hmm,' said the assistant to himself, then disappeared from the room.

Left in the fitting room, Tom tried to avoid looking at himself in the huge mirror opposite him, but he felt compelled to. His fur was pale ginger and had none of the lustre that the assistant's fur had. His claws were ragged, dirty and blunt from working in the orphanage, and his eyes were a dull brownish amber. There was no way the assistant could mistake him for anything other than what he was: a poor orphan cat. What was he to do? Was he to stay here in his underwear, waiting for the assistant to reappear and throw him and Zachariah out of the shop, or say that there was nothing here that he could afford, which was accurate? Tom had just started to pull his trousers back on when the assistant reappeared, his arms weighed down with garments. He stared at Tom with a puzzled look, then caught himself and regained his professional stance.

'If sir would like to try these on and then join Mr Black in the salon,' he said, before hanging the garments up and withdrawing.

Tom took the first suit down. It was of the deepest midnight blue material, more soft and fine than anything he had felt before. He slipped on the trousers and then, unbuttoning a white wing-tipped shirt, eased it on before putting on the matching double-breasted waistcoat and tailcoat. The lining was of emerald green, with just a fleck of gold running through it. Tom looked at himself in the mirror only to see a young gentlecat looking back – one he had not seen before.

He stepped out of the fitting room and stopped in front of Zachariah who was chatting amiably to the assistant. At Tom's appearance they both stopped talking and turned to him.

'Well, look at you, Tom Angel,' said Zachariah. 'You look like a proper gentlecat now.' He stood up and walked around Tom. 'Yet again you have surpassed yourself, Alfred. We'll take it!' he said to the assistant, who thanked him and left.

'Zachariah!' Tom said in an exasperated whisper. 'I can't afford this. I can't possibly afford this!' He started to remove the jacket when Zachariah put his paw on his arm.

'It's my gift to you,' he said, 'and I'll hear no more about it. Anyway, Claudia would want you to have the best, so the best you'll have.'

Tom started to protest again but was shushed by Zachariah as the assistant returned.

'Alfred, could you also send a few more suits, hats, gloves and undergarments, you know the sort of thing, to my aunt's house, for Mr Angel here? Whatever you think would suit him. Thank you.'

The assistant nodded in acknowledgement and handed Tom a small, beautifully wrapped package containing his suit from the orphanage.

When they left O'Neill's, the sun was sparkling on the pavements, its heat warming their fur.

'Shall we head home?' Zachariah asked, popping his cane under his arm.

'Home, yes,' Tom said. And for the first time in his life, he felt he was going home.

Two

They lounged in Zachariah's rooms that afternoon, dozing in the sun and then looking out over the enclosed gardens of the square. There was a quiet knock at the door and Agatha came in and curtseyed.

'Sir, there is a gentlecat to see you.' She curtseyed again, handing a business card to Zachariah. 'Shall I show him in?'

Zachariah looked at the card and smiled. 'Yes, yes, show him in, Agatha. The gentlecat is here to see Tom, not myself.'

Tom's ears pricked up at his name. Who could be here to see him? No one knew he was here. He half-stood up to greet the gentlecat, as in walked a slim, silver Devon Rex with the most extraordinary facial markings Tom had ever seen. It looked as though he had a handlebar moustache curling up from his lips into his cheeks, and the fur on his head had been fashioned into a peak in the middle of his ears.

Tom extended his paw to welcome this newcomer. The cat held it firm and twisted it round to see Tom's claws.

'Yes, yes, you are correct. There is a lot of work to be done here,' he said, looking sidelong at Zachariah. 'It is not an afternoon's work, but I can begin at least.'

Zachariah smirked and nodded.

'Tom, let me introduce you to my barber and groomer, Tarquair. I'm afraid I neglected to tell Tom I was expecting you, Tarquair, so I do apologise for the shocked look on his face. I asked Tarquair to pop over and give you a bit of a spruce-up.'

'Lovely to meet you, Tarquair.'

Tarquair held Tom's paw firmly between his own. 'Your knowledge is scant, but much is expected of you, little one,' he said.

Tom pulled his paw away and looked over at Zachariah who shrugged. When he looked back at Tarquair, he was busying himself over a large doctor's bag from which he pulled assorted brushes and combs. It was as if the exchange hadn't taken place, but Tom could still feel the cold rush that had shot down his spine.

He flicked his tail in agitation, but Tarquair seemed completely oblivious to the discomfort he had caused.

'Please take your clothes off and wrap yourself in this,' Tarquair said, throwing a thin wrap to Tom without looking up. 'Hurry.'

Tom dashed into his bedroom and removed his beautiful new suit, placing it carefully at the end of his bed. Then, tying the wrap in a knot around his waist, he returned to the sitting room.

'Sit, sit. I will begin,' Tarquair said, ushering him towards a leather club chair in the middle of the room.

Tarquair set about with great gusto, tugging at Tom's fur, trying to unknot fur that had been matted for as long as Tom could remember. He began with a paddle brush, with little metal prongs to undo the tangles, then once he had established that Tom had fleas as well, a slim comb and drops were produced, and much to Tom's humiliation, Tarquair proceeded to deflea him in front of Zachariah. The pair of them delighted in counting the fleas as he killed them one by one, but by the time they got into the mid-twenties they gave up. There were just too many to count. Once Tom had been declared defleaed and tug-free, Tarquair set about cleaning and sharpening Tom's claws. When he had finished, Tom ached from top to tail. Every part of him had been pummelled and pulled, and every strand of fur ached. Tom reached for the wrap, eager to cover his scrawny ginger body, but Tarquair wagged a manicured claw at him.

'No,' he said, and with a nod of his head, sent him to the bedroom to retrieve his new suit.

Tom ran with his tail down and his ears flat. Had he not had enough humiliation for one day? Swallowing down tears, he quickly changed and returned to the sitting room where Zachariah and Tarquair were now standing at either side of the large ornate fireplace.

'Now, this is better,' said Tarquair, bouncing on his hind paws and manoeuvring Tom in front of a full-length mirror that had been brought from Zachariah's room. 'Now you are a gentlecat.'

Tom stared at his reflection. He didn't recognise himself. His ginger fur gleamed blonde and gold. Bold stripes like angel's wings ran across his cheeks. The grubby fur on his chin was now a perfect little white goatee, giving him an air of age and sophistication. His claws had been tamed, the cuticles pushed back, and talons buffed and sharpened to perfection. Half-turning, he looked at his tail – it was no longer scruffy and matted but silky and smooth, and for the first time it was perky, standing upright from his beautifully-cut suit. Even his eyes seemed brighter; bright crystalline amber instead of their normal dull brown. Tom was speechless and could only stare at Zachariah and Tarquair.

Zachariah was rocking back and forth on his hind legs, his tail swinging wildly behind him. He was grinning from ear-to-ear.

'Happy?' he asked. 'You'll give me a run for my money with the queens now, no doubt. Tarquair, you are a miracle worker. I owe you one.' He gripped the cat's paw between his own, smiling at him.

'I have only opened the door to the cat he is to become,' Tarquair said. 'He will face many enemies and battles before time has passed.'

'Okay, old man, whatever you say.' Zachariah thanked him again and walked him to the door as Tom stood still, looking at his reflection in the mirror.

'Thank you, Tarquair,' he said, locking eyes with him in the mirror.

'Master,' Tarquair replied, bowing to him as he left the room.

Zachariah flung himself into his seat by the fire and started hee-hawing with laughter.

'Oh, masterful one, tear your eyes away from yourself for one minute and come and sit down, will you. I'm sitting here looking at your tail.'

Tom turned and smiled at him and sat in the chair opposite.

'What was that all about? Is he like that with everyone?'

'He's quite a cat for using his sixth sense is our Tarquair, but I've never heard him spout quite so lyrically before...' Zachariah took a poker and gave the coals a prod. 'Strange.'

Tom gazed into the glowing embers and unconsciously began to purr. He wondered what Tarquair had meant.

They spent the rest of the afternoon dozing by the fire. Tom was in the middle of a wonderful dream about a lilac-furred temptress when a noise awoke him with a start. Agatha was standing beside Zachariah shaking him gently.

'Sir, Mistress Claudia says to tell you that dinner will be served in ten minutes.'

'Thank you, Agatha,' Zachariah replied, stretching his whole body in a long sinuous arch and rubbing his whiskers with his paw.

'Right,' he said, half-yawning, half-meowing, when Agatha had left, 'a quick brush up and we'll head downstairs. Claudia likes me to be on time.'

They reached the dining room just as Agatha placed a silver platter of food onto the centre of the table. The room was now bathed in candlelight, and Claudia was seated at the top of the table as before. The soft glow of the candles made her fur sparkle and glint, making her look as though she were made out of pure molten silver. Silver candlesticks adorned the table, reflecting the chandelier overhead and making the room look as though a million stars had exploded in it.

'It's beautiful,' Tom stuttered, gazing up at the ceiling, watching the lights refract around the room.

'Come on now, Tibbles,' laughed Zachariah. 'Don't get all "chase the sparkles" on me.' They both laughed although Tom found it hard to pull his eyes from the room and focus on his dinner companions.

Dinner was a sumptuous affair. Tom had no idea who did the cooking in the household, but they cooked with a divine touch. The poached salmon starter was cooked to perfection, and the roasted rabbit melted in his mouth. After the crème anglaise dessert he thought he had died and gone to heaven. This time last night he had been in the orphanage, just another hungry little kitten, and yet twenty-four hours later here he was wearing the finest clothes and dining on the finest food in Edinburgh.

Claudia and Zachariah chatted easily, and Tom sat back and watched them. Although they had been separated for years, they were easy and comfortable in each other's company. Tom wondered why they would offer such hospitality to him. Claudia had let this strange young cat into her house, offering her home with open arms and warmth, and asking nothing in return. It was true he had looked after Zachariah when they had been in the orphanage together as kittens, but everyone knew that no matter the bond inside that awful place, you could be separated in the fraction of a second it took for adoptive parents to select you, and you would never see your friends again. How he had hated those days when the bell clanged and they all had to line up in the yard, awaiting the once-over from the visitors. Time and time again he had been passed over: "We're not looking for a ginger." He could hear the words now and felt the sharp sting of another heartbreak inside him. Zachariah was the same. No one wanted black cats either. "Too plain, or too creepy," the visitors would say, as if the kittens couldn't hear them, and Tom's heart would break for Zachariah too. He remembered the day that Zachariah had left. They had stayed in their basket longer than they should have, but they didn't want to be parted. Zachariah had come of age six months before Tom and, although he knew it was inevitable, Tom didn't want his best friend to leave. There had been lots of, 'We'll keep in touch', and play-fights, while trying not to think about the reality of being on the streets trying to fend for yourself; but the time came, and when the governess came in and told Zachariah to leave, Tom could barely look at him. His last memory had been of Zachariah standing at the door, turning back, just as it slammed behind him. And here he was now, laughing and joking with his aunt, and using all that boyish charm that he had with the queens. Black cats are most definitely not plain and creepy, Tom thought.

'And what of your family, Tom? Do you know anything about them?' Claudia's voice brought him out of his reverie.

'Very little. I was handed into the orphanage as a kitten. My parents are dead, that's all I was told. I don't know anything about my extended family. I suppose they must be out there somewhere, but I wouldn't have any idea where to start looking. The only possession I have is a locket. It's very precious to me. It has a picture inside, I think of my mother. She was a beautiful cat.' He stopped, the words catching in his throat.

'I'm sure she was,' said Claudia. 'Her son is one of the most beautiful cats I've ever laid eyes on, and I've met a few!' She laughed, looking over at Zachariah. Tom blushed to the tips of his fur.

The next day blazed bright and clear through the curtains of Tom's room. He yawned and stretched out his whole body, his muscles creaking and complaining. He lay back in the sun and closed his eyes and tried to remember the dreams of the night before. He had had them his whole life, the same dreams over and over – warrior cats fighting in lands that he didn't recognise. Just an active imagination, he thought, as he stretched out again. There was a knock at the door and Zachariah entered, a newspaper under his arm.

'Morning, Tom. How are you on this bright and sunny morning?'

'I'm good. What time is it? I need to get out there and find a job. I can't impose on your hospitality any longer.'

Zachariah waved the newspaper at him. 'Claudia likes you, my old son, and that means you don't need to worry about things like that. Besides, being a working cat isn't safe these days.'

He threw the newspaper onto the bed. Tom lifted it up and saw a headline on the front page that read, "Missing Cats' Bodies Discovered". Underneath a photo of a police cordon was the story: Two missing cats were found yesterday, dumped on waste ground outside Aberdour. The cause of death was, as yet, unknown, said a police source. Organised crime was suspected of the killings.

Tom put the paper down and looked at Zachariah. 'Organised crime in Aberdour? A bit unlikely, isn't it?'

'The world isn't safe these days, my lad. You're better off being a cat of good fortune.' He licked a spot of cream off his tie. 'Anyway, Claudia says she wants us to meet a fellow she knows today, a Felix De'Ath.'

Tom's eyebrows shot up. 'Felix De'Ath? Lucky Death? Is that some kind of nickname or what?'

'Oh, I never thought of that,' Zachariah laughed. 'Anyway, we're meeting him in an hour's time, so get a shake on.' With that he left the room and let Tom attend to his daily grooming.

The address where they were to meet Mr De'Ath was a private townhouse a few streets along from Claudia's. They were shown into a spacious orangery by an elderly cat of an indeterminate colour, being a mix of brown and beige. The room was warm and welcoming, and they sat nervously making jokes until he arrived.

Felix De'Ath was the most impressive cat Tom had ever set eyes on. By birth he would have guessed him to be Burmese, but there were mixes of other breeds in there too. His colouring was of the deepest rich ruby chocolate and his eyes, the clearest blue Tom had ever seen, were hypnotising. He was muscular, tall and very intimidating.

'Gentlecats,' he said, holding out his paw to Tom. 'Good to meet you.' His pawshake was firm and friendly.

'You must be Tom Angel,' he said smiling, 'and you must be Claudia's nephew, Zachariah. Welcome, welcome!'

He eased himself into a chair opposite them and lifted up a jug. 'Would anyone like a glass of milk, or cream?' They both shook their heads in unison.

Zachariah cleared his throat. Evidently, even he was intimidated by Felix. 'My aunt asked us to come and meet you here today, sir, but she didn't tell us why.'

Felix put the jug down and leaned back in his chair. 'These are troubling times,' he said. 'Now, more than at any time in our history, we are in danger. Dark forces are gathering, and we need to protect ourselves. You may smirk, little ones, but it's true. Can you not feel the chill in the air, that unexpected tingle in your whiskers when you're walking past someone? Oh yes, it is happening. Claudia knows – she remembers the last time we fought. It was in the Far East then, and we managed to beat them back into hiding. This time...' He shook his head with weariness. 'I'm not so sure this time. It feels different, but I don't know why. They have more energy, more of a focus.'

'Excuse me sir, but who are "they"?' asked Tom, his voice tenser than he had hoped.

Felix for a moment focused on his face, then smiled. 'The Cait of Ce. They are after power. Dark power in all its forms. Their leader, Kasperi, died recently and they are now ruled by his daughter, a ruthless queen. Recently the Ce have become more callous, they don't seem to care who they kill or what the consequences are. The rumours are that the queen is after something that, if she possesses it, will allow her to become the most powerful queen ever known. Whatever the truth of it is, they are certainly becoming more arrogant in their actions.' Felix shook his head and scratched at the back of his ear. 'These latest killings are just a calling card. There is no illusion about who is responsible. It's got the mark of Ce all over it.'

Tom could feel the fur on his back stand on edge, and he could see his tail starting to fluff up in anticipation of the danger.

'The who of what?' asked Zachariah, whose voice was calm, but Tom could sense the tightness in his body. 'And why does Claudia want us to meet you?'.

'The Cait of Ce are an ancient cat clan, based in the north of Scotland, and Claudia wants you to be able to defend yourselves, so you don't end up like those poor cats in Aberdour.' Felix ran a claw along a fine black whisker. 'And she wants me to show you both how.'

The tension in the air was almost palpable. Tom could feel his heart beat in his throat, and his tail, although he was holding onto it tightly, was becoming fluffier by the minute.

Zachariah smirked. 'No offence, sir, but what could you show Tom and me that we won't already know? We were brought up in the orphanage, you know. Life was tough. It was a cat-eat-cat world.'

The words were barely out of his mouth before Felix pounced on top of Zachariah and, pinning him to the floor with his body, sank his teeth into his throat. Zachariah hissed and flailed about, his mewls weak under Felix's grip on his throat. Tom could see Zachariah's eyes searching frantically about, but he felt transfixed. Was he

35

going to see his friend mauled to death in front of him? Felix slowly removed his fangs from Zachariah's throat, but remained gripping him with his paws.

'Deep breaths, little one. You'll be okay. I didn't even break the skin.' Felix smiled at Zachariah, their faces still inches apart. 'You feel a bit calmer now?' Zachariah nodded. 'I'm about to let you go. Try to fight your instinct to take a swipe at me.'

They both sat back on the floor, Zachariah holding onto his throat, panting, his tail and back-fur on end. Felix sat opposite him, picking bits of fur from his teeth.

'Still think I can't show you a trick or two?' Felix laughed, his breathing heavy. 'Poor old Tom here never even got out of the starting blocks.' He patted Tom on his leg. 'I'm not sure we would want him on our side in a fight.' Felix stood up and ruffled the fur on Tom's head, which Tom then had to hastily rearrange with use of a paw and a lick of spit.

As Zachariah settled back into his seat, Felix poured them all glasses of milk.

'When I say we fought in the Far East, I really do mean we *fought*. It was tooth-and-claw stuff and not all of us returned. It wasn't just China mind, but Nepal, India, the whole of that region. Cats were plentiful and poor. They were easy to recruit to the Ce's cause. Just tell the poor beggars what they wanted to hear, that they would become rich beyond their wildest dreams, feed and clothe them, and they would be yours to do your bidding.' Felix shook his head. 'I don't know if it will be all that different this time round. Times are tough, and there is many a cat on the streets who shouldn't be. And there are those who will do anything for anyone for the promise of food and a warm bed for the night.' He took a long drink of his milk. 'That is what we are fighting against.'

'But why us?' Tom blurted out. He was still holding onto his tail.

'Claudia wants to protect both of you and to know you can look after yourselves, if you ever need to.' Felix looked into his empty glass and swirled the dregs around, then looked up at them. 'Anyway, isn't it a good thing that young gentlecats about town can defend themselves?'

Felix put this glass on the table and got up. He indicated with his paw for Tom and Zachariah to follow him.

Leaving the orangery, they headed towards the front of the house before Felix stopped at a solid wooden door at the end of a corridor.

'Whatever you see here, stays here, you both understand?' he said.

THREE

Felix took a key from his pocket and unlocked the door. Leading the way down a spiral staircase, he quickly disappeared from view. Tom and Zachariah glanced at each other warily, then followed. The stairs creaked as they wound their way down, the light from the hallway growing dimmer. At the bottom of the stairs, they found themselves standing in a large circular antechamber. Like the rest of the house, it had richly coloured wooden panelling and the floor was an intricately designed mosaic depicting what looked like cats in various wars and fighting stances. There were gaslight sconces at intervals in the wall, and although they were not lit, the room was bright. At several points, doors were inset into the panelling. The room was cool and calm.

'Welcome, young sirs, to the Games Room of the Order of The Cataibh.' The last word came out half as a word, half hiss from Felix.

'The Order of the what?' asked Tom.

'Cataibh, Tom. It's a region in the north of Scotland. It means Kingdom of the Cat.'

'So what's this Order of the Cataibh got to do with the Cait of Ce?' Tom sprayed Zachariah with spit trying to pronounce the words and apologetically brushed it off his coat with his paw.

'It goes back hundreds of years. It all begins with a king who ruled over all of Alba, as Scotland was then known. This king, Cruithne was his name, had seven kittens. He gave each of them a region of his kingdom to rule over. Five of the kittens were peaceable, but one brother and sister hated each other. She wanted more power than her region of Ce had afforded her. She wanted her brother's region of Cataibh as well, and so fought him for it. She won the battle and her brother fled, ending up in Edinburgh with a few loyal followers. He formed the Order of the Cataibh. His sister claimed the region of Cataibh as her own, but the clan name of Cait of Ce remained.'

'So, you're a descendent of the tom cat who got his tail whipped by his sister?' Zachariah asked, barely concealing the smirk on his lips.

'Yes, Zachariah, you could say that, although I like to think we've held our own in the battles with the Ce since then,' replied Felix.

'And you're still fighting each other after all these years?' asked Tom.

Felix nodded, 'The Cait of Ce are power hungry. They will stop at nothing to achieve it. Kasperi was a good cat, and we have had peace between the Ce and the Order for many years, but his daughter is a whole different furball. She is most definitely a descendent of the first queen of the Ce. There will be battles ahead, so this is why we must train for them. Here in our headquarters.'

'This place is amazing, Felix.' Zachariah said, turning around on the spot, trying to take in their surroundings. 'So where do all the doors lead?'

Felix tapped the side of his nose. 'All in good time, little one,' he said.

'The battles ahead?' Tom stammered. 'What battles? And why is this called the Games Room?'

Felix leaned against the door frame and it creaked under his weight. 'As I already said, we have fought before, and I know we will have to fight again in the not too distant future. Be rest assured that when the Cait of Ce fight, they will be fighting to the death. With every ounce of their being they will do whatever it takes to get to their goal, to achieve supreme power. And, little one, this is known jokingly as the Games Room as you will play to every strength you have and a few you didn't know you had, and when you think you have exhausted every way you can think of to hurt, kill and torture your opponent, we will show you some more. There are no "games" to be had here, at least not in the traditional sense.'

'Great, where do we sign up?' Zachariah smiled, rubbing his paws together.

'You, little one, were signed up the moment Claudia found out you were alive. She told me you were a strong, fierce warrior just like your father, and you, Tom Angel, are now part of our little family too.' Felix stroked his whiskers and held Tom's gaze. 'You have to believe in yourself, Tom. You're much more of a warrior than you think.'

Tom could feel himself starting to blush under his fur, and he glanced away from Felix to take in the room.

'You know what, Felix, you're the second cat who's told old Tom here he is a cat to be reckoned with. I'm beginning to wonder about you - you keeping some deep, dark secret from me, Tom?'

Tom shook his head and smiled at Zachariah. 'I'm just an orphan with good friends.'

'One day you may need those friends, Tom, and if you are as loyal a friend to them as you would hope they are to you, then you will be a very lucky cat. Trust in them. You may owe them your life one day.' Felix reached out and put his big muscular paw on Tom's shoulder. 'I know a good, strong warrior when I see one, and that's you.'

They stood in a moment of awkward silence before being interrupted by the butler entering the room.

'Excuse me, sir, but Mistress Claudia has telephoned. She is expecting the young gentlecats home for lunch and was enquiring as to whether you were all finished playing here?'

Felix laughed a deep hearty laugh. 'Yes, we've finished "playing" here. Tell Claudia she can expect her charges home for lunch and all in one piece, so far.'

The butler nodded and left. They could hear his pawsteps slowly plodding their way back up to the ground floor.

'Well, young gentlecats, we can't keep a queen waiting, now can we?' said Felix, gesturing towards the staircase.

'Not Aunt Claudia anyway!' said Zachariah, as he took the steps two at a time.

Felix joined them for lunch at Claudia's and throughout he and Claudia flirted with each other. Tom sat watching them, fascinated by their chemistry, and he felt an ache in his heart. No one had loved him the way these three cats seemed to love and verbally play with each other, and he longed for their familiarity. Felix might have said Tom was part of the family now, but he still didn't feel that way.

After a light lunch of poached chicken and greens, Tom and Zachariah walked back to Felix's house with him. At his door they stood chatting, simply passing the time of day about what was happening in the world around them.

'Well, I must take my leave, little ones. Come over tonight,' said Felix, shaking their paws. 'The Order meets when the moon is full, and I want to introduce our two newest members to everyone. They will be pleased to meet you both, at long last.'

They took their leave and headed off into an unknown future.

FOUR

After dinner that evening, Zachariah and Tom retired to their rooms. Tom felt sick with nerves and could hardly undo the buttons on his suit to change into the more sporting attire that Zachariah had bought that afternoon for both of them. Zachariah seemed buoyant about the meeting that night at Felix's house and chatted on about what the evening would be like, as Tom trailed behind him, dragging himself into a shirt, waistcoat, tan breeches and brown lace-up boots. They both donned sports jackets for the walk ahead.

Out in the street, Zachariah bounced along the road, shadow-boxing and pouncing on any leaf or insect that flitted past them.

'Come on, Tom, where's your sense of adventure?'

he shouted over his shoulder as he wiggled his tail and jumped onto a sycamore leaf with all four paws. 'It's just a bit of fun. I mean you don't believe all that nonsense that Felix De'Ath gave you, do you? Claudia wouldn't let us get involved in anything dangerous.' He jumped up at a moth, catching it in his front paws.

'It all sounded real to me, Zachariah. I mean those deaths were real and the things Felix told us about that other clan sounded plausible, and what about that room he took us to? That was real.'

'Tom Angel, you are a big cat's blouse! That secret society of his will turn out to be a gentlecats' club and we will all sit about all evening drinking cream and making small talk. You mark my words.' He put a paw around Tom's shoulder and hurried him along the road.

The butler they had met in the afternoon opened the door, ushered them into the warm entrance hall and took their jackets. Zachariah smirked at Tom as he handed over his jacket to the cat and rocked back and forward on his paws humming a tune to himself.

'This way, sirs,' said the butler, beckoning towards the staircase. They walked down the stairs into the previously brightly lit Games Room to find it was now lit by the gaslight sconces in the wall. In the flickering light the cats in the mosaic floor now seemed to dance and fight, and Tom could feel the fur on his back and tail start to tingle and lift in anticipation and fear. Felix emerged through one of the doors in the room and Tom immediately jumped, his tail fluffing in fright.

'Tom, Zachariah, good to see you both,' Felix said, with a warm smile and an outstretched paw. 'Come meet the other members of the Order. Shepard! Jones!'

Two cats emerged from out of the gloom. They were big, muscular cats and Tom only came up to chest height on the one called Jones. They all shook paws warmly and made idle chat whilst the rest of the cats gathered. Tom noticed Tarquair, their groomer, on the other side of the room. He nodded to Tom but carried on talking to the cat he was deep in conversation with.

Once the circular room was filled with cats, Felix walked to the centre and lifted a paw to silence everyone. Immediately all the cats stopped and turned to him.

'Gentlecats, I wish to introduce you all to the two newest members of our little cats' club here.' There were a few ripples of laughter throughout the room. 'This is Tom Angel and Zachariah Black. I want you all to welcome them with open paws.' Several cats came up to Tom and Zachariah and shook their paws or patted them on the back, introducing themselves.

'Let's get down to business, shall we?' said Felix, breaking the camaraderie. 'Shepard, Jones, do you want to show the little ones what you're made of?'

46

The two cats nodded, discarded their waistcoats and took up a stance in the middle of the room. Instantly, the other cats backed towards the wall of the room as Shepard and Jones started circling each other, their eyes locked, a low growling coming from both of them. Tom could feel his hackles rising and a tightness in his throat. He glanced at Zachariah and saw his eyes widened, pupils dilated, and any pretence of bravado gone. He looked as scared as Tom felt. In a split second the fur was flying. Shepard and Jones had each other in a vice-like grip around the head, and Jones was kicking Shepard's head with his paws. With lightning speed, Shepard turned so that Jones was under him and locked his jaws around his throat. Jones let out a small mewl, then before he knew it, he had his teeth in Shepard's belly, his feet kicking wildly at his head. As Shepard's head bounced back and forth in time to Jones's kicks, he squirmed again and was on Jones's back, his teeth in the scruff of his neck. Tom could hardly breathe, watching the scene in front of him but managed to drag his eyes away from the duellers to take in the rest of the cats. They were standing around, watching, briefly chatting about this and that to a companion or two, and Felix even had his back to the fight. With an enormous thump, Shepard and Jones landed at Tom's feet, still each in a death grip with the other. Beside him, Zachariah let out a painful mewl that echoed around the room. In an instant, Shepard and Jones parted and were beside them.

Felix flew across the room at the same time to their side.

'You okay?' asked Shepard, in between pants of breath. He leaned over and rubbed a stitch in his side.

'I thought he was going to kill you!' Tom exclaimed. His voice was a high-pitched mewl.

'Nah, we were just having fun!' replied Jones. His fur was glistening with sweat and he too was panting.

Felix took one look at the expression on Tom's face and started laughing. It seemed to be a laugh that started at his toes and bounced off all the walls.

'Shepard, why don't you show Tom a few moves? Jones, you take Zachariah here. I don't want them to get the wrong impression about us on their first trip here.'

Tom glanced at Zachariah then followed Shepard into one of the rooms off the main room and found it well lit and encased in padded walls.

'Practice rooms,' Shepard said in explanation. Tom nodded, still mute.

For the next few hours, Shepard took Tom through the basic moves and holds and showed him where his weaknesses lay. It seemed that all those years of trying to scrap his way through the orphanage, he had been fighting the wrong way; like a flitty queen, as Shepard put it. By the end of the night his fur was sweaty and stuck to his face and body, and he ached from all the pummelling he had taken from Shepard's paws. When he emerged, the main room was bright and empty, the other cats having left some time before. Zachariah was sitting slumped on the floor, his back against the wall. As Tom entered, he looked up and eased himself to his hind paws.

'Let's go,' he said, 'before that damned Jonesy shows me any more of his tricks.'

The next few weeks were full of trips to the Order's secret room and more aches and pains than Tom could cope with. At times both he and Zachariah practically fell through the door at Claudia's and could barely bring themselves to drag their weary carcases up the stairs to their rooms. The only thing that kept them going was the regular newspaper reports of disappearances and deaths along the east coast of Scotland. Over the last few weeks they seemed to be getting closer to Edinburgh. Initially it was disappearances, then a few days later the bodies would turn up. Every time Tom read of another poor cat meeting his or her end he felt sick and could only hope that the little they were doing with the Order would help in some way.

One bright morning at Felix's they sat chatting in the orangery.

'I just feel like I'm doing nothing. We are leaving those poor cats to die horribly,' Tom said.

'We are doing our best, little one, but yes, we have lost a few good cats already,' Felix replied. 'Don't be so hasty to get to the fight. We only play-fight here. Remember, when you face the Ce warriors, they will be fighting to the death, and they won't worry about preserving your good looks.' He laughed, but Tom could tell that even he was worried.

'I don't think Jones is worried about preserving my good looks in the slightest,' said Zachariah. He was sporting a rather magnificent scratch right across his forehead, which had removed some of his eyebrow.

'I think you'll find the queens will still love you with a scar or two. In fact, it might add to your charm.' Felix laughed, and this time Tom had to agree with him.

Everywhere they went in Edinburgh, Zachariah drew admiring glances from female cats, and Tom could see why. His coat was so silky and beautiful that you wanted to reach out and touch it. He walked with his head held high like he owned the entire street, and he looked like a cat with a pedigree going back hundreds of years. No one would have guessed they were both street-cat orphans. Tom, on the other hand, may have looked like a gentlecat, but he still felt like that unwanted kitten deep down, and worse still, he was invisible to the queens who flirted with Zachariah.

That evening, as a full moon rose over the city, the whole Order met again. Once more they dressed in their sporting attire, although after a month's wear, and fighting in the rooms, they weren't looking quite as swish as they had on that first night. There was a nip in the air and Tom pulled his collar tight around his neck for warmth. As they walked the short distance between Claudia's and Felix's homes, Tom felt his fur prickle and his ears shot up to listen. Immediately Zachariah noticed the change in his stance. He too pricked up his ears and turned his head slowly to catch their silent companion.

'Can you see anyone?' he whispered under his breath.

Tom gave the smallest shake of his head. He moved his eyes to scan the gardens lining the street opposite and saw a slight motion near some trees. He shot across the road, Zachariah in hot pursuit behind him, and he could feel the muscles in his body tense into fight mode. Leaping over the iron railings and landing in the ghostly still gardens, he stopped dead. Zachariah landed softly beside him. The moon lit the frost on the grass and made the shadows in the trees dance.

'Over there,' Tom whispered to Zachariah, indicating the expanse of grass. Pawprints dusted the surface of the frost, heading off into the darkness of the distant streets.

'Let's check it anyway,' Zachariah replied, moving stealthily forward, his paws barely leaving prints on the ground.

Tom followed behind him, his eyes aching with trying to focus on the dark corners of the trees. After a few minutes' hunting he could feel the adrenaline ease from his body, and he shouted to Zachariah, 'Let's go. There's no one here now!'

Zachariah appeared out of the shadows, shaking his paws, which were wet from the frost. 'We'll be late if we don't hurry anyway,' he said, vaulting back over the railings and adjusting his jacket.

As they walked off at a brisk pace, Tom glanced over his shoulder, a cold chill making him shiver.

Deep from within the canopy of the trees, two yellow eyes watched them walk down the street and into the warmth of Felix's house.

The butler, whose name Tom now knew was Ash, greeted them warmly. 'Good evening, gentlecats. The master is waiting for you downstairs.'

They handed their jackets to him and made their way down to the now familiar room. This evening the room was bright, the sconces unlit, and Felix was conversing with Shepard, their heads together. As Tom and Zachariah walked in, Shepard said something to Felix and he turned to face them.

'What happened?' was all he said, his eyes bright blue, scanning from Tom's face to Zachariah's.

'I think we were followed,' Tom answered.

'Did you see them?'

'No, but I sensed them. I knew we were being watched. We gave chase into the gardens, but whoever it was got away.'

Felix's face grew tight, his whiskers quivered. 'Never do that again,' he said, his voice tight. 'You come straight here, you hear me?' Tom nodded.

Shepard touched Felix's paw and said in a quiet voice, 'They thought they were doing right, Felix - leave them.' Felix glanced at him and then back at Tom, but he spoke to Zachariah.

'Why don't you and Tom tidy yourselves up? We've got a new member joining us tonight and I don't think you want to give the wrong impression.' Then he turned and walked from the room without a backward glance.

When Zachariah and Tom returned to the room, it had been filled with familiar faces. Cats stood about chatting, waiting for the evening to begin. Felix strode into the centre of the floor. As usual when Felix spoke, silence descended.

'Tonight, we have a newcomer to the Order. I would like you all to welcome Meissa. She knows only too well the ruthlessness of the Cait of Ce. Meissa, would you like to tell everyone your tale?'

A petite lilac Burmese mix with piercing green eyes walked into the centre of the room to stand beside Felix. Tom felt his stomach do a flip as she flicked her gaze to him then away again.

'My mother and father were both killed by the Ce,' she said in a clear voice. 'A month ago, they were taken from their home, tortured, then murdered. I found their bodies in a ditch not far from our home.' Her voice quavered. 'I vowed that day to avenge their deaths and I will fight with every ounce of my being to do so. Friends of my parents knew of the Order, and here I am.'

Felix put a paw on her tiny shoulder. 'You are one of our family now, little one.' She looked up at him and smiled, and Tom's stomach did another flip. 'Enough talk, on with the games,' Felix bellowed. The main lights dimmed, the sconces burned bright and Meissa was taken into one of the rooms to begin her lessons.

Zachariah and Tom stayed in the circular room with a few of the other cats. They had progressed, albeit slowly in Tom's case, from paw-to-paw combat to fighting using their other senses. This made them stronger as a team as they could anticipate what their opponent was going to do before they did it. Tonight, however, Tom's mind was filled with Meissa and he found it impossible to focus on what his opponent was about to do to him, meaning he ended the night having taken a pummelling. He was just glad he hadn't been partnered with Zachariah – he would have humiliated Tom all the way home, and Tom would never have heard the end of it. As the evening ended, Tom kept glancing towards the door where Meissa had gone at the beginning of the evening.

'Looking for someone?' asked Felix from behind him, a sly grin on his face.

'No, no,' Tom replied, feeling the blood rush to his face.

'She's left already, little one,' Felix said, whispering in his ear. 'But don't worry. I have a feeling you'll be seeing a lot of little Meissa.'

Tom felt Felix's paw on his shoulder briefly, but when he turned, he was gone.

FIVE

'Find him and bring him to me!' Sophia let go of the cat she had been holding by the throat, and he ran from the room. She clattered her claws against each other, and a low growl emitted from her unwittingly. Since her father had told her that Thomas Angel was alive, she had had only one focus – to find him and kill him. And now it seemed he had disappeared. What was wrong with these cats that they couldn't find one pathetic little kitten out there in the world? She stood up and began to pace up and down the room, trying to think through her options. One of her warriors approached, bowing deeply before her.

'Don't,' she said, 'unless you're about to bring his carcase into this room right now. Just don't.'

He left the room without another sound.

The room grew dark around her and still she paced up and down. She could wait – anyone who had seen her stalk and kill her enemy knew she would bide her time, and when it came, she was ruthless in her precision. She looked around at her surroundings. The oak-panelled room had seen the births and deaths of generations of cats. The stories it could tell, the secrets it kept – battles had been fought and won here, and now it was hers, and she would do everything in her power to keep it that way. Anyone who crossed her once would not live to try it a second time. She had one focus and one love, and it was the Cait of Ce. The clan was her blood, her fur, her very soul, and no thing or cat was going to take it away from her.

The warrior crept back into the room and cleared his throat. Sophia started.

'We have news of Thomas Angel, mistress.' He kept his eyes on the ground.

Sophia moved towards him until her face was inches from his. The smell of fresh blood was metallic on her breath. 'And?'

'He is living in Edinburgh with a cat named Claudia Black.'

At the sound of that name Sophia hissed into the face of the cat. 'Get out!' she spat into his face, taking him by surprise.

He backed out of the room, scared to turn his back to her in her rage. Sophia slumped into a seat and began to weep.

The next day was misty and cold, and a fog swirled around the broch. Sophia stirred in her bed. Her sleep had been long in coming then filled with night terrors of the past and the future. To rule the Cait of Ce was her birthright; she came from a long line of clan chiefs. No one would take it away from her. The stronger the lineage of the leader the stronger their power would be. Sophia was the tenth generation of the same family of cats to rule the Ce, and she was determined that her power was not going to be taken away from her. She had been taught in the ways of the warrior as a kitten, always knowing that one day she would rule the Ce, and she would do everything in her power to keep it so. She thought of Kasperi, her father whom she had adored and admired. He had been a peaceable leader, but that was not her way. As long as the Order opposed her and her Cait of Ce she would never have the power she desired, but once she had crushed it, and she would, then nothing would stand in her way. Now the Order was protecting Thomas Angel – well, that gave her another reason to annihilate it, and annihilate it she would. Not only was the Order of the Cataibh the hated enemy of the Ce, but now that they had Felix De'Ath at their head and were hiding little Thomas, her pleasure would be all the sweeter when she killed both of them. Stretching herself to her full length, she got out of bed and yelled for her maid.

'Bring me my warriors,' she said.

With her warriors assembled, Sophia entered the meeting room of the broch. The stone tower had stood for thousands of years, passed down through generation after generation of cat. She inhaled and felt comforted by its familiar smell. A taut silence descended, and a chocolate tabby cat shifted in his seat nervously. Sophia raised a claw and glanced at him. He stopped moving.

'What news?' she asked, her glittering amber eyes scanning the cats.

'None so far this morning, other than the update I gave you last night, mistress,' replied a gold-coloured cat, holding her gaze.

'My plans have changed,' Sophia said, walking behind the cat who had spoken. 'Forget about Thomas, for the moment. Now we know where he is, I can take him any time I choose. I want you to find out everything about him, his friends, confidantes, loves, whomever he comes into contact with. I will hunt him down, but first I want to play with him, weaken him, make him vulnerable. Then I will strike.' The golden cat nodded. 'And, Flynn, stop your warriors from killing cats. We know Thomas's where-abouts, and we don't want to make it too obvious we're after him.' The golden cat gave a sharp nod. 'That goes for all of you. If there is killing and torture to be done, I'll be doing it. Do I make myself clear?' The cats nodded.

'Then go!' said Sophia, dismissing them like kittens.

Six

'It's too quiet,' said Felix. He was sitting with Claudia in her library. 'I don't like it.'

'Hmm, it makes you wonder what she's up to.' Claudia turned away from the window. She sighed. 'We have to give the kittens their freedom. It's no use cooping them up in here.' She walked over, sat beside Felix and took his paw in hers. 'You know them – we can't stop them from being kittens. They are enjoying their freedom after spending all that time in that awful Orphans' Hospital, and Zachariah will look after Tom. He thinks of him as his brother, you know.'

Felix gave a little laugh and looked down at the floor. 'It's Tom I worry about,' he said. 'He just seems so, I don't know, so young and helpless.'

'Zachariah will look after him. Stop worrying.' Claudia squeezed his paw as a cacophony erupted in the hallway.

At once Felix was on his feet and halfway to the door just as it burst open. In tumbled Zachariah, Tom falling on top of him, both with canes in their paws and hooting with laughter. They both yowled with hilarity until they caught sight of Felix's enormous hind paws at their heads. Realising who was standing there, they both bolted upright to a standing position.

'Sorry, Felix, we didn't know you were here,' Tom mumbled, looking at his paws and feeling himself go red. 'We were just play-fighting.'

Felix looked at both of them sternly, then he started laughing. It was a deep, hearty laugh that seemed to come from the pads of his paws.

'Well, don't let me stop you,' he said, ruffling the fur on Tom's head, still laughing. Claudia got up from her seat and walked Felix to the door, and Tom could hear the pair of them still laughing as they said their goodbyes. He looked towards Zachariah and shrugged.

The next night was the first time they had been back to Felix's house since Meissa had come to the Order. Tom took longer than normal to get ready and brushed his fur until it practically glowed.

'You okay in there?' shouted Zachariah, thumping on the bathroom door. 'Or have you drowned?' Since that first day when Zachariah had taken him shopping, Tom seemed to have acquired rather a lot of toiletries. As well as the requisite flea powder, just in case, you understand, he now possessed glosses for his whiskers, shimmery pomades to make his fur glisten and all manner of implements for claws – to buff them up, keep them trimmed and push the cuticles down. To be perfectly honest, he wasn't exactly sure what some of these things were meant to do, but the assistant in the shop had assured Tom that he needed them. Tom had a sneaky suspicion that it had more to do with Zachariah flirting with her than any concern about Tom's facial fur.

'I'm coming,' Tom called, with one last brush and check in the mirror. That would have to do, he thought as he opened the bathroom door in a cloud of perfumed steam.

They arrived at Felix's house in plenty of time for the start of the evening's proceedings to find Felix and Jones deep in conversation. Tom had almost flung himself down the now familiar stairs, anxious to see Meissa again. Felix spun around at his entrance.

'Ah, good evening, gentlecats.'

Jones nodded and then went back to speaking to Felix. Tom glanced around the room in search of Meissa, but she wasn't there yet.

'Looking for anyone in particular?' asked Zachariah, a sly smile on his mouth. 'A particular queen, that is?'

'Just wanted to see who was here, that's all.'

'I asked her out.'

'You what?' Tom's voice was louder than intended, and Jones looked around at them. Giving him a weak smile, Tom turned back to Zachariah. 'Why?' It came out more of a mewl than he had hoped for.

Zachariah shrugged and leaned back against the wall, his paws in his pockets. 'Thought she was quite pretty and you'll never get anywhere if you don't ask,' he said, although he averted his gaze.

'You knew I liked her. I told you!' It came out as a pure mewl. Tom could feel a growl building deep in his throat. He didn't know if he felt hurt, angry or betrayed, or all three.

'Sorry.'

At that moment, Felix called for quiet and the room fell silent.

'We believe the Cait of Ce have changed tactics,' he said. 'They seem to have gone to ground, and we all know only too well it's not like the Ce not to trumpet their arrival in town.' A few laughs echoed off the walls of the room. 'We don't know what's happened to change things. We believed they were after something – whether that's changed or not, I'm not sure, but certainly they no longer seem to be seeking it.' He glanced over at Jones. 'Just be aware of who you speak to. They, like us, have spies everywhere, and no one can be trusted. I'm not saying there are spies among us here – just be wary, watch your back, and keep your mouth shut.'

The air prickled with energy, and Tom could feel his hackles give another little spike.

'Right then, enough tittle-tattle. On with the games. Meissa, Tom, I'd like you to go head to head in the main room tonight.'

Tom turned his head to find Meissa standing between Zachariah and himself, smiling up at him.

'I do hope you've been practising. I don't take prisoners,' she said, slipping off her jacket and making a few little jumps and swiping moves with her delicate paws. She was wearing, instead of her usual full skirt, a pair of fitted tan breeches and lace-up brown boots. Tom's heart did a flip.

Zachariah slapped him on the back and snorted, 'Good luck, mate. I think you'll need it.' Tom could feel the anger return, and he wished it were Zachariah he had to fight and not petite little Meissa.

'Come on!' she shouted from the centre of the circle, beckoning him in.

The other cats had once more lined up around the outer walls of the room, and the gaslights had been dimmed. Tom took a deep breath and walked up to face Meissa. Suddenly he was on the floor, staring at two cats holding each other's tails on the mosaic, and Meissa's paw was on his back between his shoulder blades.

She leant down and hissed in his ear, 'Fight me.'

Tom struggled back to his paws and almost immediately Meissa grabbed him round the neck and was pulling him back down to the floor. An instant after that, he was flat on his back staring at the ceiling, and Meissa was straddling him, her paws lashing out at his head. He managed almost to reach a crouch when she kicked him in the side, and once more he was on the floor, staring at the same two cats with their tails in their paws. As he turned over to get up once more, Tom saw Meissa raising her paw to kick out again, but he grabbed it and brought her down on the floor beside him. This time it was she who was struggling to gain her paws as Tom leapt on her back, his claws round her throat. He shoved her face towards the floor. As she lay there, apparently lifeless, he started to panic. He released his grip slightly – and she had him, once again, pinning him underneath her. He managed to wriggle round and nipped her on her lower back with his teeth; he felt her yelp in pain. She soon made him pay for the move as she quickly turned and sunk her teeth into his ear, and this time it was he who yowled loudly. Meissa let go quickly, a look of surprise on her face, and Tom took advantage of her momentary weakness to sink his teeth into her throat, pinning her beneath him. In return, Meissa took her claws and twisted them into his stomach, catching a nipple. Tom reacted by curling up, holding his stomach and panting. He realised Meissa was lying next to him gasping for breath too. He looked over at her and their eyes met. Her pupils were dilated, with the smallest tinge of emerald green showing around them. It felt to Tom that he lay there for hours staring into Meissa's eyes, but it must have been only seconds, as Felix strode over and unceremoniously pulled Tom up by the scruff. Once Tom was standing, Felix went to Meissa and helped her to her paws, leaning in to speak to her.

'Gentlecats, the winner!' Felix laughed, holding Meissa's paw aloft. She winced at the movement but looked over at Tom and smiled. He smiled back, and his heart flipped.

The next day when they returned to Claudia's for lunch, Tom and Zachariah could hear voices and laughter coming from the sitting room. On entering, Tom was pleased to see Felix but delighted to see Meissa. She was sitting beside Claudia who was holding her paw and chatting to her like they had known each other for years. As they entered, both Claudia and Felix looked up and smiled. Felix stood up and nodded a welcome to

Zachariah, but swiftly took Tom by the elbow.

'I'd just like to have a little chat with you,' he whispered in his ear. 'Claudia,' he called over his shoulder, 'we won't be long.'

Tom glanced back as he left the room only to see Zachariah sitting down next to Meissa and taking her paw in his.

Felix walked with him to the library, looked quickly around, opened the door and entered.

'Sit, he said. Tom sat. 'I wanted to be the one to tell you Tom, before you heard it from someone else in the Order, but it seems that the Cait of Ce have targeted you. We're not sure why, but they seem to think you're a direct threat to their organisation. The hierarchy are keeping the real reason close to their chests'.

Tom put his head in his paws trying to take in what Felix had just told him. It made no sense.

'Why me Felix. What have I ever done to them? I'm nobody.' Tom's voice cracked as he spoke, a combination of shock, confusion and dread coursed through him.

'Believe me, my cats have tried to get the information out of them as to why you, but I can't ask them to put themselves in danger just for us.' Felix hunkered down in front of Tom and put his paws either side of the chair. 'I promise you with all my heart I won't let them get you. They'll have to get through me first.'

'I can't let you do that, Felix!' Tom started. 'I'll try harder to be a better warrior. You can teach me. Please, Felix, I couldn't live with myself if anything happened to you!' Their faces were inches away from each other.

'And I couldn't live with myself if anything happened to you, little one. You remind me of myself when I was a kitten.' Felix smiled. 'So, you want to be a big bad warrior like me?' He stood up. 'Well, you're going to have to be able to react to this!' And with that he made a series of pats on Tom's head, ears, paws and chest.

Tom flailed about, trying to bat Felix's paws away but failed each time. Finally, Felix ruffled Tom's fur and dragged him to a standing position and pulled him into a brief hug.

'Let's eat – we need to build up your scrawny little body if you're going to take me on.' Felix put his paw around Tom's shoulder and walked with him back into the dining room where the others were waiting.

Lunch was, as usual, a sumptuous affair with a seafood platter of several fish and shellfish Tom had never seen before, and on Felix's insistence he accepted seconds. Throughout the lunch Zachariah sat beside Meissa, whispering into her ear and making her laugh or blush in equal measure. Tom tried not to let it bother him, but he could hardly hide his disappointment that Zachariah would do this to him when he knew he liked

Meissa. When Felix suggested that Tom might accompany him back to his house, Tom eagerly accepted his invitation. As they walked the short distance they chatted amiably, Felix regaling Tom with tales of the adventures he had had. When they reached Felix's familiar front door, Ash opened it for them. Tom smiled; he felt like he was home.

As he followed Felix down the now familiar staircase to the Games Room, Tom felt all his senses stir. He felt a throb of fear in his throat and his hackles tingled and lifted slightly – it wasn't just the thought of paw-to-paw combat with Felix. As the feeling grew to a tingling all over his fur, he shivered and fought against the sensation. Entering the antechamber, a pawstep behind Felix, he noticed that it was as Felix lifted his paw that the lighting changed from bright to the sconce's soft gaslight.

'This way,' said Felix, turning a key in a door off the main room.

The room was, like all the others, circular with padding on the walls and an intricate mosaic floor. The gas-lit sconces bathed the room with the same gentle flickering light as before, and the mosaic cats danced in the glimmering lights. Tom followed Felix into the room before Felix locked the door from the inside.

'Now, little one,' he said, 'so far you have been learning to fight with tooth and claw but fighting the Ce won't be as easy as fighting little Meissa was the other night.'

Tom blushed, thinking about having been beaten by her.

'They will use all their senses, and if they are targeting you, you must be ready to fight them at their own games. You must continue to learn, to fight with your heart and with your soul. It won't be easy, mind, but the things worth fighting for never are. Are you ready, little one, for your lessons to begin?'

Tom nodded, too terrified to speak.

Felix raised his paw and the lights went out in the room. The darkness was suffocating. Tom couldn't even see his paw in front of his face, and he had to swallow to stop the palpitations throbbing through his veins.

'I want you to close your eyes, Tom. Just close them and breathe for me, slowly and deeply. With each breath in, I want you to breathe a bright, white, multifaceted light into your soul - feel its warmth deeper and deeper into your bones, your muscles, your blood. Feel that white light shining outward into the darkness. Can you feel it?'

Tom nodded, keeping his eyes firmly shut. His thumping heartbeat had disappeared, replaced by a warmth and calm that felt like a warm blanket being wrapped around him.

'Good. Now I want you to focus that white light on this point here.' Tom felt a claw gently touch between his eyebrows, where his fur darkened to look like a letter

71

M. 'Focus on this point. Feel the light travelling from every inch of your soul until it focuses at this point, like a spotlight. Now try to direct the light into the darkness. Can you see me now?'

Concentrating on the light radiating out of his forehead, Tom imagined seeing into the room they were standing in. At first everything was a dark, smudgy, grey, but as he forced himself to think of nothing else, the room came into focus, slowly lightening and clearing as he concentrated. He could see Felix standing a few feet away from him. It was like being in a swirling fog that lifts suddenly, letting you see clearly. Felix was standing as clear as day before Tom; a strange turquoise glow seemed to emanate from him.

'Well done. Now I want you to find the walking cane that Ash so kindly placed in here for me. Turn slowly round and find it and bring it to me.'

Tom turned his head quickly and the fog swirled round him. He couldn't see anything at all. It left him with a queasy feeling in his stomach, and his head gave a painful thump.

'Gently,' said Felix's disembodied voice from behind.

Tom tried again to focus on centring the light and clearing the fog, and after a few moments looking around tentatively, he saw the cane. Tom walked slowly over to it and bent down to pick it up. To his surprise the cane felt heavy and strangely real in his hand. He looked down, amazed to see his own paw wrapped around it.

'Now hand it to me,' he heard Felix say.

Tom turned more slowly this time, and although he could feel the darkness encroaching at either side of his sight, he managed to hold it at bay as he walked cautiously towards Felix and handed him the cane.

'Well done, Tom!' Felix said, smiling. 'Now I want you to once again think about the white light, but this time, think about it becoming less powerful. Slowly close it off from your M, your third eye, and then breathe it down through your body and into the ground. Can you do that for me?'

Tom nodded and was overcome by the queasy feeling again. He imagined the white light disappearing, and eventually he stood there in the dark with his eyes closed.

'Open your eyes,' said Felix, and as Tom opened them, he started. The room was still pitch-dark and he had no idea where Felix stood.

'But I could see!' he said into the darkness. He heard Felix make a movement and the sconces flickered into life. Tom blinked in the dim light.

'That was your sixth sense, little one. You used the power of your soul to see, when in reality you shouldn't have been able to. I'm so proud of you. It took me weeks before I could pick up a cane.' Felix placed his paw on Tom's shoulder and smiled, his eyes glistening. 'So proud. You are a very special kitten, Tom. Now, let's go have a seat and a glass of cream. I think you deserve one.'

Over the next few days Tom saw hardly anything of Zachariah or, for that matter, Meissa. Every time Zachariah was in their rooms at Claudia's, Tom avoided him, and when Tom was in there, Zachariah was nowhere to be seen. At least Zachariah had the decency to avoid speaking about Meissa and himself when he and Tom did come across each other; Tom was at least grateful for that. Tom spent most of his time with Felix at his house and, although he was fond of Claudia, he grew closer and closer to Felix. Tom looked forward to his chats and Felix seemed pleased to see him, although after so many disappointments in the orphanage, he still held himself back, not wanting to be hurt. He practised strengthening his sixth sense, and he couldn't wait to show Felix how he had improved.

One morning, a couple of weeks after Tom started practising with Felix, Felix greeted him warmly with a hug at the door, with no sign of Ash.

'Come on, little one, I want to show you a new trick today,' he said, reaching for Tom's paw before he even had his tailcoat off. They ran down the stairs and into the room once more; it seemed welcoming and homely to Tom now.

'Today we are going to focus on using your seventh sense.' Felix grabbed Tom's tailcoat and flung it onto the floor.

'I didn't know I had seven senses, Felix. Mind you, I didn't know I had six senses until two weeks ago!' Tom laughed, picking up his tailcoat from the floor and folding it into a neat square. It hadn't been so long ago that he hadn't had such a beautiful item as that tailcoat, and although he wasn't speaking to Zachariah at the moment, he was still very grateful for his love and friendship.

'Well, little one, you are about to learn all about it. Your seventh sense is based on universal energy, just in the same way as your sixth is intuition and second sight. You are going to use your white-light energy to your advantage. The power is within you, always remember that. Now watch.'

Felix raised his paw and aimed the flat of it towards Tom's tailcoat lying neatly on the floor. The tailcoat started to move and unravel itself, then it rose into the air. Tom stood open-mouthed, unable to believe what he was seeing. He couldn't take his eyes off the now hovering coat, although he also desperately wanted to see what Felix was doing. The coat moved towards them, only faltering once, when Felix sneezed, and then came to rest on Tom's shoulders as though it had been sitting there all the time. Tom turned to face Felix, eyes and mouth wide open.

'How, what, how?' he stuttered.

'I used my energy, little one, and you can do it too. It can be very useful in a cat fight. You can protect yourself and use it against your enemy. And it's all there inside of you. It's part of your being, and if you harness it properly you can become a very powerful warrior.'

Tom shook his head. 'Felix there is no way I can learn to do something like that. It was amazing!'

'Parlour tricks, little one, that's all that was. It's within you now – you just need to know how to use it. Now take your tailcoat off again and get yourself comfortable. This could take a while.'

They stood in the darkened room facing each other. On Felix's command, Tom closed his eyes and started breathing deeply as before. As he breathed in time to Felix's breathing, he started to feel the white light glowing in his stomach. The warmth and the light got stronger and stronger until he could feel it pulsating through his body. Energy effervesced through his veins, and he could feel the heat it was generating.

'Tom, I want you to feel the energy moving down your arms and into your paws. Can you feel it?'

'Yes.' Tom could feel the energy undulate from his chest into his arms and down into his paws.

'Good. Now stretch out your paws in front of you and feel the power and heat move through your paws and into the air in front of you.'

Tom did as he was told. Suddenly, he was aware of a pushing against his paws.

'Open your eyes,' said Felix.

Felix stood about two paws' length away from Tom. He had his paws outstretched and a white sparkling light was coming from them. It seemed to be pushing against the light coming from Tom's paws and, as the two lights combined, they glittered a rainbow of colours. Astonished, Tom lost his focus for a split second and was flung across the width of the room, only to land with a thump against the opposite wall.

Felix came rushing over to him and gathered him into a big bear hug.

'That was the most splendid first attempt to harness the power I've seen in a long time!' he said, momentarily releasing Tom in order to look at him before then gathering him back into a hug. 'Well done, little one, well done.'

'Thanks,' Tom replied, rubbing his rear end, 'but can I wait until my tail recovers before I attempt it again?'

Felix laughed and hugged him again.

SEVEN

Sophia stood on the broch roof, looking out over the heather-covered mountains. She felt refreshed by the cold air whipping through her fur.

'Is this my destiny, Kasperi?' she wondered aloud. 'To stand alone, always alone, and stare out at these damned hills? Was I wrong to do what I did? Did I have any other choice than the path I chose? I wonder. All I want is the best for us, for the Ce, but now... I don't know. You would never have wavered in your path, I'm sure of that. These cats might see me as the weaker sex, but I know differently. I know I'm more powerful than they will ever dream of being, more than most of these fools even desire to be. I am the beating heart of the Cait of Ce. It is my calling. I will never let you down. I will not let the Ce down. But those cursed dreams... Night after night they follow me through the hours of darkness, mewling and crying through the dark until the sun rises once more. How many more nights can I endure them? How long must I bear them? Thankfully they do not follow me through my days, when I must be clear and lead the clan, but the nights are so long. Kasperi, help me forget them.'

Flynn stood at the crest of the stairs leading to the roof. In the distance he could see Sophia standing by the edge. She was muttering to herself again and looked weary. What disturbed her soul so? After Kasperi's death she momentarily seemed to blossom; as he breathed his last, so she seemed to prosper, but now? Now she seemed to crumble with every day that passed. Flynn rubbed his ear. What would be her next move?

She sensed him behind her.

'What is it, Flynn?'

'Your warriors are waiting for you, Sophia. I can dismiss them if you...need more time.'

'I'm ready.'

The Ce warriors had been summoned to the meeting room. A fire blazed in the grate; they warmed themselves in front of it, their tails swishing this way and that in the heat. Sophia entered the room, her black cloak billowing behind her.

'Well?' she said, walking directly towards them.

'Thomas Angel is spending the majority of his time at the Order's headquarters with Felix De'Ath,' Flynn replied, striding alongside her. The other cats stood to attention immediately when they realised Sophia was there.

'So, what is the plan. How to do we get rid of my little problem?' Sophia looked around them, but they all seemed to be busying themselves finding something interesting on the floor to look at. 'You, speak,' she said sharply to a grey tabby. He looked uneasy at having to speak to Sophia directly.

'Mistress, we have found a number of his acquaintances from the orphanage and my soldiers have dealt with them according to your wishes. However, none of them were able to tell us anything we didn't already know about Thomas Angel. He is friends with a black cat with the name Zachariah. They are now both living with his aunt, a Claudia Black, and she seems to be connected with the Order and Felix De'Ath, both of whom I believe you already know about.'

Sophia hissed in the grey cat's face, spraying spit all over him. 'Then find out something I don't already know about!'

Flynn stepped between them, affording the cat a defence. 'They seem to have befriended a queen. Our spies have seen her in their acquaintance on more than one occasion. You had us "interview" her parents, mistress. I believe they had fought for the Order last time, in the Far East. Their name was West – you may remember them.'

Sophia took a step back from the grey cat and met Flynn's gaze. She wrinkled her nose and put her head to one side as she considered the name.

'No, I don't think I do remember them, but there were so many cats then. After a while, they all blurred into one,' she said, dismissing the Wests with a flick of her paw. 'Those were the days, weren't they, Flynn? We had so much fun, didn't we? All those cats hanging on our every word, our very thoughts, eager to do whatever Kasperi and I wanted them to. Then that damn Order had to go and spoil our fun. If it weren't for the likes of Felix De'Ath and Claudia Black I would be mistress of all I desired, not stuck out in this godforsaken wilderness, trying to keep warm and keep my little clan together.' Sophia's expression softened, and her eyes sparkled as she remembered happier times from long ago. She seemed caught in the past and totally unaware that she was standing in a room with a dozen warrior cats, all awaiting her instructions. She pulled her cloak around her for warmth and turned to walk out of the room. At the door she paused, her back still turned to the cats.

'Flynn!' she called back. 'Find the West kitten and bring her to me!'

*

Claudia was woken by shouts in the house. Panicked, she reached for her dressing gown and ran out into the hallway.

'Agatha!' she called out. 'What's happening?'

Agatha came tearing across the landing, holding up her skirts as she ran. 'It's the young gentlecats, ma'am – they are growling and hissing at each other.' She glanced up the stairs to the third floor where noises could be heard. 'I don't know how to stop them, ma'am. I think they will come to blows.'

Claudia left Agatha trailing in her wake as she tore up the stairs to Tom and Zachariah's rooms. She flung open the door to find them in a heap on the floor, scratching and hissing at each other. Grabbing a jug of roses by the fireplace, Claudia flung the whole lot over both of them, and with an instinctive reflex they both separated and shot to different sides of the room. The room looked a state, covered in water and crushed flowers, with bits and pieces flung everywhere. Claudia stood in the middle, so they would be unable to start fighting again.

'What are you two up to now?' she shrieked. 'You woke me up, and I hate being woken up!'

Tom looked at the floor fully ashamed of himself. He wanted to crawl behind the sofa and hide. Claudia and Zachariah had been kind enough to offer him their hospitality and this was how he repaid them.

'I'm so, so sorry, Claudia,' he said. 'I'll pack my things immediately. I've let you down. Sorry isn't enough, sorry.'

'Oh, do be quiet, Tom, and stop apologising. Cats will be cats. Now, what are the pair of you fighting about?' Claudia sat down on the floor between them and looked to Zachariah and Tom for an answer.

'It was nothing,' said Zachariah, still looking at the floor. He was wearing a crown of crushed roses.

Claudia cocked an eyebrow. 'Tom?'

'We were fighting about Meissa, that little kitten. I like her, and so does Zachariah, and I guess I just got a bit jealous of Zachariah. He, he...' Tom stopped. He didn't know how to say that he hated the way Zachariah had everything and he had nothing, and he couldn't even allow him to have someone to love of his own; he had to take that too.

'I shouldn't have rubbed your nose in it, Tom. Sorry.' Zachariah brushed the flowers from his head and they fluttered to the floor in front of him. The way he wasn't looking at him, Tom could tell that he felt the same way about the fight. They might both be saying that it was about a female kitten, but they were both harbouring grudges against each other over something entirely different. Tom just didn't know what Zachariah was angry about.

Tom had nothing that he didn't already have in triplicate.

'Come here both of you,' said Claudia, stretching her paws towards them. They remained where they were. 'Shake on it.'

Reluctantly, Tom and Zachariah reached out and shook paws.

'There we are. All friends again.'

Even Tom could feel the distinct frostiness that still stood between himself and his best friend.

The next night it was the first evening of the full moon and the next full meeting of the Order. Tom asked Zachariah if he was going, but he told him he was meeting Meissa, so Tom dressed in his usual attire and walked the familiar route on his own. As he walked, he could feel a set of eyes watching him from the gardens, but this time he didn't chase and challenge them. He just put his head down and carried on walking towards Felix's.

Tom was standing in the Games Room talking to Shepard, his back to the entrance, when a ruckus caused all the cats in the room to turn and face the door. In a split second the atmosphere changed, and the room was full of cats primed for fighting. With a last few thumps and bumps, Zachariah landed on the bottom step on his back, tail askew and fluffed up. Tom ran over to him, all previous arguments forgotten for the time being, and helped him to his paws.

'What's happened?'

'She's gone.'

Tom knew at once that Zachariah meant Meissa.

'Claudia?' said an anxious voice beside him, and he realised Felix was there.

'Meissa,' was all Zachariah said.

Tom's stomach knotted, and he heard a little mewl escape from his lips.

'What happened, Zachariah? Take your time.'

They were now sitting in Felix's spacious library, surrounded by his inner circle, consisting of Shepard, Jones and Ash. Tom was sitting on the other side of Zachariah, not really knowing what to do with himself, and suppressing the urge to shout at them all to stop doing nothing and get out there and look for Meissa.

Zachariah rolled the glass of warmed cream Ash had given him between his paws.

'We had arranged to meet up in town at that milk bar on George Street – you know the one?' Felix nodded, and Tom looked at him, surprised that he would know where a trendy milk bar was. 'We had finished our drinks and were walking down Frederick Street, heading towards here, when from somewhere in the gardens I heard a noise and before I could turn we were set upon by a pack of cats.'

'How many?' interjected Shepard. He had a little wrinkle between his eyebrows.

Zachariah looked up at him, perplexed. 'I don't know – five, maybe six. It all happened so fast. Before I even had the chance to get my claws out, there were two of them on top of me, holding me down, and I could hear Meissa yelling and fighting as she struggled with them. I couldn't see properly as a big ginger tom was sitting on my head.' He glanced over at Tom and smiled. Tom smiled back. 'All I could hear was Meissa yelling and cursing them as they hustled her away through the gardens. The two holding me down made a leap for the trees and had disappeared before I got to my paws. I tried to go after them, but they were long gone. I don't even know what direction they went.' He stopped and stared into the middle distance, his glass still between his paws. 'I'm sorry.'

'We've got cats out looking for her. Don't worry, we'll find her.' Felix placed a paw on Zachariah's shoulder.

'What if we don't?' exclaimed Tom.

Felix turned to him, meeting his frightened eyes. 'All we can do is our best, little one. That's all we can do.' Tom nodded as he felt a surge of energy race through him. He trusted Felix to find her.

'Shepard, go and find out where they have taken her, although I think we can all probably guess where.

Tom, take Zachariah's other arm. We'll get you home and let Claudia know what's happened.'

As they walked along the street like a strange six-legged cat, carrying Zachariah between them, Tom leant across and whispered to Felix.

'Felix, I want to help find Meissa. She's a friend, Felix. We can't just let the Cait of Ce take her like that.'

Felix smiled. 'Little one, I won't let your friend down. We'll find her, and you will be there by my side – don't worry about that. I need my best warriors with me, don't I?' Tom felt himself go redder, embarrassed that Felix knew that he had feelings for Meissa.

As they approached the house, Claudia ran out to meet them, gathering them all into her arms.

'Thank goodness you're all safe!' she said, giving them all kisses on their faces. 'I was so worried when Ash called.' She pulled them all into another hug.

'We're fine, Claudia,' said Felix. Tom could see that, for once, he was a bit discomfited by this show of affection. 'Let's just get the kittens into the house where it's safe and then I'll tell you all about it.'

The next morning was grey and dreich. As soon as Tom woke and remembered last night, his stomach lurched. He must have fallen into a sleep at some point in the night, but images bounded through his head of Meissa, a shadowy presence chasing after her. More than once in the night he had reached out his paw to try and grab her, only to wake up with an empty paw and a cold sweat on his fur. He practically fell out of bed and out of his room, only stopping to grab his dressing gown. As he lurched into the sitting room, he almost fell over Zachariah who was lying flat out on the floor in front of the now dead fire. He sleepily opened an eye and tried to focus on him.

'Meissa?' he said, and then realising his mistake, rubbed his eyes and sat up. 'Is there news?'

'I don't know. I just woke up,' Tom replied, their animosity to each other forgotten. 'I'll grab your robe for you.' He went into Zachariah's darkened room and picked up his dressing gown. By the time he got back to the sitting room, Zachariah was standing and stretching.

'Surely Felix would have told us if they had found her?'

'I'm sure he would,' Tom replied, holding out the robe for Zachariah to put on.

They took the stairs at a trot and fell over each other trying to get into the dining room at the same time.

Felix and Claudia both looked up from their newspapers.

'I know it's kippers for breakfast, little ones, but no need to fight to get them. There's plenty for everyone.'

Felix meant it as a joke, but it fell flat as they both tried to speak at once. He raised his paw.

'If I had heard anything about your friend, don't you think I would have been straight up those stairs to tell you?' he said. Now that Tom looked more closely at him, he saw that Felix looked tired, and bags had formed under his eyes overnight. Claudia too looked as though she hadn't slept.

'Come now, Tom, Zachariah, sit down and eat something. You'll need to keep your strength up if we are to help Meissa.' Claudia looked from Tom to Zachariah. 'Both of you. Now, sit.'

As they tucked into their kippers, Felix filled them in on what had happened the previous night.

The night before, Felix told them, Shepard and a few others had set off to find Meissa and her kidnappers. They had followed their trail to a disused dock in Leith where they had lost the scent.

'We think they may have taken her to the Ce lair,' he said. 'I'm waiting to hear from there at the moment, but my friends within the Ce have to be careful, especially now.'

'Why now?' asked Zachariah, his kippers in pieces in front of him.

'Because they will start to suspect everyone of being traitors if they find out we know anything, and the consequences of that for my friends, well...'

The sentence hung in the air, but he didn't need to finish it. They had all seen the photographs of what the Cait of Ce had done to other cats, innocent cats at that. Who knew what they would do to one of their own if they caught them spying for the Order?

'Can't we at least make a start for their lair, Felix?' Tom asked. He wanted to get Meissa back as soon as possible and he didn't want to think about what she was going through right at that moment.

'We will. Just as soon as I have word, little one. Don't fret, we will get her back.' Felix glanced at Claudia, and Tom knew from her look that even she doubted his words.

For the rest of the morning Tom paced from room to room, not knowing where to put himself. He spent most of the time in the sitting room, which looked out into the street, just searching for a familiar face, but for once every cat on the street was a stranger. He hadn't seen Zachariah since breakfast, and Claudia and Felix seemed to continually have their heads together anytime he glimpsed them on his travels through the house. He was just completing another circuit of library, sitting room and dining room, when he happened upon Felix coming from the kitchen. Tom looked at him expectantly, waiting for news.

'Nothing,' he said, shaking his head. Tom let out a half-mewl, half-sob. Felix put his paw round his shoulder and led him into the sitting room.

'Talk to me, Tom,' he said. 'You'll feel better for it.'

Looking into those intense blue eyes, Tom took a deep breath.

'I think I love her, Felix,' he said, and then halted in surprise at what he had said. He considered for a moment, then continued. 'I love Meissa. I mean, I know I don't know her really, but you know that gut instinct you get about someone and you can't explain why? Well, I just knew I loved her from the moment I set eyes on her. And it sounds daft, but when we were fighting and she had me held down on the floor, I didn't want her to let go of me. I mean I did, because it hurt like hell, and I thought she had broken my arm, but I could smell her fur and feel her touch and I didn't want her to let go, ever.'

Felix nodded. 'You feel like you've lost part of yourself now she's not here?'

Tom nodded.

'I have this pain that won't go away, Felix, and I don't know what to do. She's with Zachariah and he's my friend, but he knew I liked her and he still went out with her. I won't lose the only cat who has ever been there for me, but I can't imagine never seeing her again. I won't think about that. What do I do? I want to be a good friend to Zachariah, but I don't think I could bear to see them together forever.' On the last word Tom took a breath; it felt like he had been holding it since he had found out about Meissa. Felix took his paw in his.

'Tom, you have to follow your heart, whatever the outcome. You will be able to bear it if you have Meissa with you. You don't get given anything in life you can't cope with, remember that. Let me tell you a tale of a very silly young cat from a very long time ago. I was deeply in love with a beautiful queen, and I mean so beautiful that I would look on her with amazement every day and wonder what she saw in me. Anyway, we came from families who were sworn enemies. But we loved each other, and as long as we stood together we thought we could cope with anything. One day, a supposed friend of mine grew jealous of my friendship with another queen – there was nothing ever in it, mind – and made it his business to tell my beautiful queen that I was betraying her with this other cat, which I wasn't. My beautiful, beloved queen confronted us, the two supposed sweethearts and when we denied it, as was correct, she flew into an incredible rage and banished us. Her family, being quite happy about this, swore to kill both of us if either one of us came anywhere near my beloved. And I never saw her again, Tom. And I wish every day that I had fought harder to be with her. To hell with what the family would have done, for from that day to this I have regretted my decision and I have never loved anyone else like I loved her.'

'So where is your beloved now? And the other female cat? What happened to her?' Tom asked.

'My beloved rules the Cait of Ce, Tom. She's not the same cat I fell in love with all those years ago though – she chose a different path. The other queen was Claudia. She was and always will be my best friend. We've been through some dark times together, but we've always been there for each other. Tom, don't lose Meissa just to keep someone else happy. Fight with tooth and claw to keep her. Don't do what I did and live your life with regrets. If Zachariah is a true friend, he will understand.' Tom nodded, his throat dry. Felix ruffled the fur on the top of Tom's head and took him into his arms in a hug.

The door opened, and Claudia entered.

'Shepard's back.'

EIGHT

All four of them skidded into the library at the same time.

Shepard sat gazing out of the window and started at their arrival.

'What news?' said Felix.

Shepard just shook his head and glanced between their expectant faces.

'No news, Felix. It's like she has disappeared off the face of the earth. Our friends in the Ce reported that Meissa was taken by them, but from there,' he shook his head, 'we just don't know. She's gone. I don't know what else to say.'

Tom slumped against the wall of books, dislodging a couple of them. Zachariah looked over at him and, finding no words, looked back over to Shepard and Felix.

'What do we do now?' he asked.

'We keep on till we find her,' Tom said, his voice stronger than he felt. Shepard looked up at him and nodded.

'I will, Tom,' he said. 'I'll keep on looking and keep on asking until I find her for you. I promise you that.'

'What can we do, Felix?' asked Zachariah, but it was Tom who answered him.

'We train, Zachariah. And we train longer and harder than we've ever done. We didn't take the Order seriously before, but now we are going to have to rely on it to give us the tools we need going forward so we can find Meissa and bring her back home safely, to us, to all of us.'

Felix put his paw on Tom's shoulder. 'Spoken like a true warrior of the Order of the Cataibh and an enemy of the Ce, little one,' he said, smiling at him.

'Shepard, go and rest. We'll need your help to find her.' Shepard nodded at Felix and left the room.

Claudia put her paw on Felix's arm.

'This isn't about you, Felix. You can't fix what happened after all these years. It's about a very scared little kitten somewhere, and our two kittens.' She glanced at Tom and Zachariah. 'You have to let the past go.'

Felix gave her a long searching look. 'I know.'

*

For the next week Tom barely slept. When he woke in the morning he had a quick breakfast at the insistence of Claudia then rushed over to Felix's house to start his lessons for the day. Zachariah's enthusiasm seemed to wane after the first couple of days of hours and hours of combat, and Tom could tell he was just going through the motions to please Claudia and Felix. That made him even more determined, and each time Zachariah seemed to lessen his efforts, it made Tom double his own. He was now becoming adept at seeing with his third eye. He could sense where everyone was in the room without seeing them in the blackness, and he was beginning to be able to anticipate their thoughts. When Tom read Felix's mind and told him to get the idea out of his head of running behind Tom in the dark to pull his tail, Felix was so proud of him he lifted Tom in the air and spun him around. Seeing they were in the pitch-dark of the room at the time, this made Tom nauseous and he vomited; so after that Felix was more reticent in his celebrations. The comings and goings of the members of the Order seemed constant, with even Tarquair showing his face once or twice during the week. As usual he bowed to Tom and called him master, much to the amusement of Felix. It was Thursday when Zachariah came across Tom in Felix's sitting room, reading a newspaper.

'Morning, Zachariah,' Tom said, trying to be civil and courteous to him.

'Morning,' Zachariah replied. He seemed a little down, but Tom held back from asking him what the matter was. Maybe he really was missing Meissa, of whom there had been no word. Folding the newspaper and placing it on the table, Tom hesitated for a moment then stood up.

'Good to see you,' he said, making to leave, but Zachariah put out his paw and caught Tom by the arm.

'Tom,' he said, then stopped. Even his voice sounded weary. 'I want to say something to you.'

Tom stopped in his tracks not sure whether he wanted to listen to what Zachariah had to say, but he could sense the pain he was feeling.

'It's about Meissa. I'm sorry.'

'What are you sorry about?' Tom asked, even though he knew the answer.

'I knew you liked her and I went ahead and asked her out anyway. I shouldn't have done that.' Zachariah paused again and looked down at his paws, which were now clasped in his lap. 'I was jealous, Tom, jealous of you and what you had, and I wanted... I suppose I wanted a piece of it. I'm so sorry. If I hadn't gone out with her that evening she might not have been taken and we wouldn't be here now. I'm sorry for everything. You were a good friend to me and look how I've repaid you. I'm disgusted with myself. I can't sleep. I think about it constantly – I'm just a mess, and all because I was jealous.' He shook his head at himself.

'You, jealous of me?' Tom said, disbelievingly. 'Me? Are you mad? Zachariah, I've been jealous of you! I had nothing before you and Claudia took me in. If it weren't for both of you, I would be on the streets fending for myself or dead in a Close somewhere. I can never repay you for the kindness you've shown me over these few months, and if it weren't for you two I wouldn't have met Felix or learned to fight like this. Yes, I like Meissa – I can't deny that – but I wouldn't ever do anything about it if you wanted to be with her. I owe you everything, Zachariah. You have nothing to be jealous about.'

Zachariah looked up from his paws into his friend's eyes.

'I'm envious of the love you have with Felix. He adores you like a son, Tom. I'm just the dandy, the Jack the Lad. He doesn't love me the way he loves you. I've seen him look at you – the little glances when you're not looking, and I just thought if I had someone who loved me like that, who loved me more than you, then I wouldn't feel as jealous. I know I've got Claudia, but she's my aunt, she had to take me in, she didn't have a choice, did she. You're nothing to Felix, and he still loves you. But it all backfired, didn't it? Meissa got abducted, and Felix has doubled his efforts with you. I'm sorry. I'm pathetic.'

Tom laughed. 'You're not pathetic, but you're a bit bloody daft! Zachariah, you mean the world to me. Don't forget, before we had Claudia and Felix there was only the two of us, facing the world in that orphanage. I'll never forget that. You'll be my best friend forever, Zachariah. No one can take that away from us. And as for Felix, well, I'm just a waif he has taken pity on. I appreciate his hospitality, but I'm not his flesh and blood. He's not my father. You're Claudia's family - that's a whole different ball game to just liking, or loving, someone. As for Meissa...' This time it was Tom looking at his paws, unable to meet his friend's eyes. 'I think I love her. And yes, I'm bloody jealous of you because of that. I've never felt like this with anyone before, and I will fight tooth and claw to get her back, but I don't want to lose you in the process, Zachariah. I would rather never be with Meissa, if you love her, than lose my best friend.' Tom reached out for Zachariah's paw and clasped it tightly. 'Can we find her together?'

Zachariah nodded, and Tom knew that all the arguing and fighting they had done with each other was over and they could focus on finding Meissa, together.

It was another two interminably long, tedious days before word came that the Ce were keeping a prisoner.

'It can only be Meissa, can't it?' Tom demanded,

pacing up and down in Claudia's drawing room.

Jones stood by the doorway. They had hardly let him in the door before they had started to bombard him with questions.

Jones shook his head. 'It could be anyone, Tom. All I found out was that a queen was being held by the Ce in Dunnottar castle, but it could be anyone. Why would they take her to Dunnottar? It doesn't make sense. If they want to torture and kill her, do it here in Edinburgh. On the other hand, if they want to extract information, or the new Queen of the Ce wants to interrogate her, they'll take her to their broch up in Cataibh. But Dunnottar? No, my senses tell me that this isn't Meissa, just some other poor kitten caught by them. I'll send a couple of cats up there to investigate.'

With that he left the room and they stood in silence whilst they gathered their thoughts. Tom was the first to speak.

'So, what do we do, Felix? We can't sit around here all week, waiting to hear whether she's alive or dead. Can't we start out for Dunnottar or this broch? At least if she is the queen we're looking for, in Dunnottar we would be right there, ready to strike.'

Felix shook his head wearily.

'To take on the Ce in their lair without a plan would be madness. No, we have to formulate a plan, to attack at their heart. It's the only way. Once they are without their leadership they will be weakened. This is all her fault, all her doing. She's brought it upon herself.'

Felix finished speaking and walked to the window with his back to them. Claudia walked over, put her paw on the small of his back and whispered into his ear. He looked at her quizzically and she reached up to touch his face and brush his whiskers. To see this invincible cat seem so vulnerable was terrifying. Felix leant down to kiss Claudia briefly on the cheek, then left the room without so much as a look backwards.

Tom stood there speechless, fighting the urge to run after Felix, to make everything be like it was before any of them had heard of the Cait of Ce. He looked over at Zachariah who had a puzzled look on his face, but he was staring at Claudia still standing by the window, and when Tom looked at her he could see the glistening wetness of tears on her cheeks and whiskers. Tom walked over to her, taking out his handkerchief, offering it to her, and it was as she dabbed away her silent tears, that a knock on the door brought them all out of their reverie. Agatha entered the room.

'Ma'am, there's a gentlecat to see you,' she said, with a little curtsey.

'Show him in.'

*

Claudia gave a final sniff into the handkerchief, pulled herself up straight and brushed down her full-skirted dress. The door opened, and Agatha showed in a tall golden cat of upright bearing. His whiskers were straight, not wayward like Tom's, and his tail was vertical, with just a little swish at the tip. On seeing him Claudia held out both her paws and he went forward and kissed them both before bending to his haunches in front of her.

'Flynn, it's been too long,' she said. 'Here, let me see you.' She pulled him to standing and then put her arms around him and gave him a huge hug, which he returned.

'Claudia, Claudia, look at you,' he said, opening her out from his arms then gathering her back into them. 'You're as beautiful as I remember.' Tom and Zachariah exchanged looks, and then they both looked back at the scene in front of them. Claudia, catching their glances, pulled away from the cat.

'Flynn, this is my nephew Zachariah and his friend Tom, Thomas Angel.' Flynn's eyebrows shot up at the mention of this name.

'Zachariah, good to meet you, and Thomas Angel, as I live and breathe! I know a certain queen who would love to be in your presence right now, and I don't think it's the one you're thinking of.' He smirked, and Tom blushed as he had immediately thought of Meissa, but if not her then who?

Claudia put her paw on Flynn's arm, stopping him from saying anything else.

'Zachariah, why don't you and Tom go over to Felix's and do some practice? I'm sure Flynn will join you later.'

Flynn nodded.

'We need to have a catch up,' she said.

Tom and Zachariah had been practising using their sixth sense against each other in the darkened room when they heard excited voices outside. The door of the room was flung open and two silhouettes were illuminated in the harsh light that flooded in. Squinting and bedazzled, Tom and Zachariah both covered their eyes with their paws. They might now be able to fight each other in the pitch-dark when they couldn't see their paws in front of their faces, but even the dim light from the gaslight outside seemed like the surface of the sun to their ill-adjusted eyes. The two figures in the doorway were of similar build and it was only when Tom heard Felix's deep raucous laugh emanating from one of them that he started to relax, and his hackles went down. Coming out into the antechamber Tom realised he wasn't the only one who was in flight or fight mode, as Zachariah was still sporting a rather fluffy tail. The second figure, it turned out, belonged to Flynn.

'Here are the little ones, Flynn. Were you enjoying

yourselves?' Felix laughed as he smoothed down Zachariah's tail. 'This is Tom's favourite game, isn't it, little one?' He put his paw in front of his mouth and said in a loud whisper that they could all hear, 'And I have to admit he's getting rather good at it. He's nearly caught me out once or twice.' He ruffled the fur on Tom's head and slapped him on the back.

'I would expect nothing else,' said Flynn, 'with a teacher like you, Felix.'

'Yes, well, come. Let's go up to the library and have a glass of milk. Flynn has the news we were waiting for.'

'You know where Meissa is!' They shouted in unison.

Flynn waved his paw in a so-so motion. 'Let's sit down first,' he said.

Tom bounded up the stairs taking them two at a time, as did Zachariah, but Felix and Flynn took an age, pausing occasionally to exchange a word or two. By the time they had reached the library and seated themselves, Tom and Zachariah were halfway through the glasses of chilled milk that Ash had kindly provided for them.

Tom drained the last of his glass and placed it on the table with a heavy clunk. Flynn looked at him and smiled.

'Yes, I know where Meissa is. The problem is not

where she is, but how we are going to get her out of there without Sophia finding out,' he said.

'Who's this Sophia?' Tom asked, as Zachariah clunked his glass on the table beside his.

Flynn glanced at Felix before answering.

'She's the leader of the Cait of Ce, Tom, and I'm one of her most trusted warriors.'

Tom's hackles rose slightly, and he could feel a growl beginning at the back of his throat.

'Wait a minute, if Sophia's the leader of the Cait of Ce, she's the one you were in love with, Felix? Your beloved wants to kill me? Why?' Focusing on Flynn, Tom demanded, 'And if you're one of the Ce Flynn, what are you doing here, with us?' Zachariah could feel the tension in his body rise too.

'I'm one of Felix and Claudia's oldest friends and yes, I'm a spy for the Order. We all knew each other as kittens. We grew up together and, well, things happened to send us down separate paths in life, but I still remember my friends. I'm not one for taking sides.'

'Yes, you are!' Tom shouted, standing up. His hackles and tail were fully on edge.

'You could have got Meissa out for us and brought her here, but you didn't. You come here with some supposed information but, it's a trap, Felix. It's one of their traps!'

Felix stood up directly in front of Tom and placed his paws either side of his face.

'Tom, I trust Flynn with my life. He has never, and will never, let me down as a friend. I'm not about to explain to you what my reasons are for our loyalty to each other. I just ask that you trust me – and Flynn. Believe me that we will both do everything we can to keep you safe. Do you understand me?'

Tom tried to speak, but Felix still had a firm grip either side of his face.

'Do you understand me?' he repeated. Tom nodded. 'Good.' He let go of his face. 'Then sit down and listen up. To answer your question, Flynn would be signing his own death warrant if he took Meissa from the Ce, and I would never let him do that. And we don't know why Sophia wants you dead. That she does means I will protect you, we all will, with our lives if we have to. Now, we have a lost little queen to bring home to us.'

Over the next two hours they put their heads together and formulated a plan. Tom felt humbled to watch these two cats, on opposite sides of the battle, come together to get his Meissa back. Instead of launching a full scale attack, Felix had said it was to be just them, making it easier to get in and out of the Broch without being detected. They had argued about whether or not Tom and Zachariah should come with them. Felix was against it, saying they were too young, and it was like baiting Sophia bringing Tom with them. Flynn had rallied to their side, declaring that they should be allowed to fight, that this is what they had trained for, to bring home their friend. Eventually, and against his better judgement, Felix agreed – much to the delight of both Tom and Zachariah. By the time they had come to an agreement it was early evening. Felix stood up and stretched.

'We leave tonight.'

NINE

It was a moonless night and Tom shivered as he, Zachariah, Felix and Flynn left the warmth of the house and stepped out onto the still streets of Edinburgh. To passers-by they looked like fathers and sons on a night out in town, but they all kept their silent opinions as they walked, weighed down by their own thoughts. They walked to Leith where Flynn had a steamboat standing by. It would take them along the coast by sea to Cataibh and the mouth of the river at Brora, which would lead them to the Cait of Ce's broch. Tom stood on the deck of the small boat as it chugged its way through black choppy waters, with lights twinkling from the coastal villages they passed. As they left the lights of Fife and headed north, the waters became wilder. It felt like an omen, like the Ce knew they were coming and were trying to stop them, or maybe it was because Tom was beginning to feel decidedly queasy. At the best of times, like most cats, he wasn't particularly fond of water, but being this close to it and for so long was making his entire body feel like jelly. Zachariah was standing beside him, his scarf wrapped round his face, whether to prevent sickness or the cold Tom didn't know. Tom tapped Zachariah's shoulder and indicated that he was heading for the cabin.

He opened the door and as the sudden heat hit him he came out in a cold sweat and bolted for the side of the boat, holding his paw over his mouth, only just managing to make it before he was sick into the foaming waters. He returned to the cabin, wiping his face with his paw, and this time managed to get himself inside and seated before the nausea caught him again. Fighting back the urge to run, he asked how long before they reached their destination. Flynn said nothing, but pushed a plate of roast beef towards him. Tom gingerly pushed it away with an extended claw, looking up at Flynn as he did.

'Eat - you'll need your strength, and Sophia isn't going to wait until you're feeling okay before she tries to kill you.'

'Have you no idea why she wants to kill me? How does she even know I exist? I'm just some kitten from the orphanage.'

'We don't know the why, just that she's decided

you're a threat to be dealt with, and when she makes up her mind...' Flynn leaned across the table to Tom, pushing the plate back towards him.

Felix looked over at Flynn, 'I told you this was a bad idea, bringing them.'

'Sophia took Meissa to lure you into her territory, so she can capture and kill you,' Flynn said matter of factly.

Tom swallowed hard. 'Why?'

'She's obsessed with being in control, maybe she thinks you're going to be more powerful than her one day, that you're going to rule the Cait of Ce instead of her.'

'She can keep her clan of psycho killer moggies. I don't want anything to do with them. Is she mad?'

'Possibly,' said Flynn with a sigh, 'and getting more unhinged with every day that passes.' He paused. 'I worry about her.'

Tom snorted in disbelief. Some mentally unstable cat, that he had never met before, wanted to kill him because in her addled brain she had decided that he was a threat to her, and Flynn was worrying about her?

'I don't think she's the only mad one in the Ce, Felix,' Tom said, making a point of looking at Flynn.

Felix smiled. 'It's complicated, little one. The strands of our lives are interwoven in ways you cannot begin to imagine. I know that Sophia, and the Ce seem to be power-crazed merciless killers, but we all have a past, and what has happened in that past makes us the cat we are today. You would be different if you hadn't been in the orphanage, or hadn't met Zachariah and looked after him, or never met me or Claudia or Flynn, would you not? Well, it's just the same with the Cait of Ce, and Sophia. If certain things hadn't happened, if the path she walked on had been a different one, well, then the four of us wouldn't all be sitting in this little boat trying to do the impossible. Don't prejudge any cat before you have lived the life they have, little one.'

'She must have had one hell of a life if that's how she's ended up then,' Tom said, shaking his head.

'She has,' replied Felix, 'and now she's lost her beloved father, Kasperi, I doubt she feels that there is anyone in the world whom she can fully trust right now.'

Flynn put his head in his paws and groaned. 'Make me feel better for betraying her why don't you Felix?' he said through his paws.

Felix put a paw on Flynn's shoulder. 'You've always been there for her Flynn, never forget that.'

As the boat chugged on through the dark night and the choppy waters of the North Sea, the three of them sat in silence, listening to the rhythmic sound of the steam engine. Tom concentrated on not being sick, but when Zachariah came into the cabin carrying a still gasping, breathing fish, he had to bolt for the side of the boat once more.

'Look what I caught!' Zachariah laughed. 'I just stuck my paw over the side and it practically jumped into my arms!'

'I think you should perhaps throw it back, little one,' said Felix. 'I don't think we'll be doing any fine dining on the boat.'

As Tom opened the cabin door after his latest bout of sickness, he heard the skipper's voice shout out, 'Land ahoy!'

'Thank goodness,' he said.

TEN

Meissa was nose to nose with Sophia in the dim, dank room. She could smell Sophia's breath, sweet and sickly. She could see her nostrils flare as she took in Meissa's scent. Meissa had been asleep when Sophia had come in and dragged her upright to her tips of her claws, and now she was holding her to her face and breathing in her smell. Meissa hardly dared to breathe. Half-asleep, exhausted and dirty, she had been kept in the room for days. She could smell the clean, fresh air outside and could just about see the stars twinkling in the pitch-black sky through a slit in the stone wall.

'So, pretty one, I can see my cats have been amusing themselves with you,' Sophia said, using a claw to trace along Meissa's face. 'Naughty kittens – I told them to keep you for me. I will have to have words with them later.'

Meissa refused to flinch as Sophia's claw arched round her eye and down her nose. As it travelled, the claw dived deeper and deeper into her fur. Sophia smiled; causing pain always gave her pleasure. Pausing for a moment, claw poised, Sophia then dug the claw into the soft flesh in Meissa's cheek.

'Do you like pain, pretty one? Pain makes us stronger.' She dug the claw in deeper. Meissa winced but refused to yowl out.

Sophia paused for a second, looking into Meissa's eyes, then pulled the claw out with a swipe. As she did so, Meissa could feel the blood welling up in her cheek and bubble up into a droplet, which Sophia leaned in to, smelled, and then licked from her cheek.

'You taste sweet as well, pretty one. Does he like how you taste too?'

'Who?' Meissa asked. It came out as a whisper.

'Don't play with me, kitten. You know who! Thomas Angel! Does he like how you taste? Answer me!' Sophia's spit covered Meissa's face.

'Tom is a friend, that's all. I don't even know him that well!' Meissa shouted, her voice becoming a squeal.

'He's a friend, is he? LIAR!' Sophia screamed, her eyes wild, pupils dilated. She was digging her claws into Meissa's shoulders pulling her tighter to her. 'I know what you're thinking and how you feel, pretty one!'

The panic started to rise in Meissa's chest. This cat was utterly mad, and she was alone in a room with her. She was going to be ripped apart like her parents and there was nothing she could do about it. Sophia put her head to Meissa's neck, nuzzled her then bit in with her teeth, the long fangs puncturing the skin. Meissa was helpless. There was nothing she could do to stop this cat ripping her throat out, and she tried to focus past the blood rushing into her ears. Sophia just held her there, her jaws clamped round Meissa's throat, teeth pressing, crushing her windpipe. Meissa started panting for breath, trying desperately to take a long lungful but unable to.

'Don't panic,' she thought to herself. 'Just stay alive.' Then just as suddenly as it had happened, Sophia let go. Meissa slumped to the floor and grasped her paws round her throat. Sophia stood over her, rubbing her fangs with the pad of her paw.

'I like you, pretty one. You remind me of myself,' she said, looking down at the kitten heaped on the floor. She opened the door of the room, but before leaving, turned back to Meissa. 'You will give me Thomas Angel though. Be in no doubt about that.'

It was beginning to get light when Meissa woke again. She had fallen asleep sometime after Sophia had left and was now curled into the smallest ball she could make to protect herself. She lay for a minute, taking stock, before she moved a paw and the pain shot through her body. She could feel the skin on her cheek swollen and tender as she winced, and trying to swallow brought on a shooting pain through her neck. Tentatively, Meissa stretched out first one paw, then another, trying to see where she hurt the most. The cats over the last few days had given her quite a few beatings, but it seemed after Sophia had been there her body had decided to let its pain be known. She stretched slowly at first then more deeply, her muscles juddering, unused to the movement. Having stretched, she tried to stand up. White-hot heat traversed her spine then her tail. Maybe I should try and work out what doesn't hurt, she thought to herself, moving each limb in turn, trying not to wince with each movement. Okay, my right paw feels fine, she thought, slowly rotating it all ways. I still have my fighting paw, that at least is a bonus. Limping over to the slit in the wall, and standing on tip-paw, Meissa could see that the dawn was beginning to break. Even in the dim light, she could see that this tower, wherever it was, was surrounded by a barren landscape with mountains soaring up either side of a loch, and a river snaking its way into the distance. Even if she managed to get out of this place, there would be nowhere to run to. There was nothing for miles. She limped back to the blanket that had covered her on her journey here and sat back down with a heavy heart. Closing her eyes, Meissa went back over the events of the last few days, seeing if she could make sense of anything that had happened to her. She thought of Zachariah and Tom, Zachariah's laugh and his sparkling eyes. He was a bit of a dandy, but that was half his charm. Tom Angel was sweet, quiet, caring. How perfect his name was for him; he really was an angel. That Felix was a rogue to make her fight him at the meeting that night, but still he gave as good as he got, and he had those eyes, those beautiful amber eyes that you could just sink into. But why her – why had she been taken? Surely if they had wanted to kill her, they would have just done so in Edinburgh. Why bring her all the way to the middle of nowhere and keep her here? And what did that female cat say? Something about Tom – what was it now? She seemed to think that Meissa and Tom were an item, not she and Zachariah. But that was just silly – and what did Tom Angel have to do with these crazy cats and this place anyway? Her head was thumping too hard to think straight, and her throat burned from the biting earlier on. She curled back into a ball. I'll just go to sleep, thought Meissa, and when I wake again it will all have been just a nightmare.

Sophia walked up the steps to reach the roof of the broch. This was her favourite part of the building. Even as a kitten she would come up here in all weathers and just look out over the wild untamed landscape. She would play hide and seek with her siblings here, hiding in amongst the stonework and thatch. That was long ago, long before she knew what it was to hate and kill, when the world was still innocent, and so was she. She sat down with her paws swinging over the precipitous edge and breathed in a lungful of the cold, sharp air. She thought of Meissa, the little queen she had as a prisoner in the jail downstairs. She reminded her of herself when she was younger, feisty and full of fight. It was a pity she would have to kill her. She was such a pretty little thing, but she had to weaken Thomas Angel. He must never find out what his destiny was; he had to be stopped. Maybe, Sophia thought, she could persuade this little Meissa to come over to the cause, to join the Ce, and stand at Sophia's right paw. She would like that, she thought; a little kitten of her own to look after, to train. She lay back, the huge expanse of pale blue sky stretching on forever.

'I could teach her everything I know.' Sophia said aloud to herself, 'But then again she might try to take the Ce from me and I would have to kill her anyway. Might as well just kill her now to save time.' She stretched her paws upward towards the sky. She could feel the chill of the air on her pads. She stretched her claws out. 'I kill her.' She said as she tucked a claw in. 'I kill her not.' She tucked another claw in. 'I kill her,' and a third claw disappeared.

118

As she tucked in her last claw, she said, 'I kill her not.' She looked at her paws in surprise, like they had somehow failed her.

Sophia lay there for a few more minutes more, gazing at the sky as it grew lighter, before she gave a final stretch and got to her paws.

'Flynn!' she yelled. 'Where are you? I need you!' She twirled around, expecting him to be standing behind her. Where had he got to? She hadn't seen him for days, she thought, or had she? All the days blurred into one at the moment. So much to do – all those cats downstairs couldn't make a decision between them. She had to do everything herself and those damned dreams kept her awake at night; she was so tired all the time. But Kasperi would be proud of her, that was the important thing – her father would be proud of her. He must be away at the moment, doing battle in the East, mustn't he? Trying to battle those damned cats who ruled there. As long as she had her father, she was fine, she thought. They were a team. Nothing would ever come between them. Ever.

The boat had moored at a small concealed wharf on the banks of the loch, not too far from the broch, just after dawn. Only too aware that they could possibly be seen, Tom and company quickly jumped onto the shingle bank and ran, crouching, into the nearby heather. Once all four of them were lying face down on the ground, the boat silently glided away from the mooring point and back into the river channel where it wouldn't be visible. Tom heard the skipper roar the engine into life away in the distance and felt very alone. Still, it was nothing compared to what Meissa was going through at this moment; she had probably already been tortured. The thought made him feel sick.

The plan was to let Flynn go ahead, with a day's head start to give him cover when he got back to the Ce, just in case they thought it was ever so slightly suspicious that he and the Order members turned up on the same day. He would then check on Meissa and give a signal to the others that she was still there and okay. Then the rest was up to Felix, Tom and Zachariah, and whilst they had planned as much as they could, so many things could still go wrong. Thankfully, as both Felix and Flynn knew the broch well, it would be easier to navigate when they got in. That was the plan anyway. Tom's stomach lurched at the very thought of having to get in there and tackle the enemy. What was he doing? He thought to himself, he couldn't do that, could he? He was just plain old Tom Angel from the orphanage. A movement to his left distracted him from his musings. He'd seen Flynn disappear into the undergrowth only to appear seconds later a couple of hundred yards away. Slowly Flynn inched forward, as though stalking unseen prey, then he darted away again, and Tom lost sight of him instantly. Scanning the distance to see where he would reappear, Tom caught sight of a shape he thought was Flynn. He was in the totally opposite direction from where he should have been. Tom watched until he could no longer make out the course of travel and settled down in the warm heather to snooze alongside Zachariah, who had been asleep for quite a while and was muttering to himself in his sleep. Every now and again his paws would twitch as though chasing and catching something.

As Flynn approached the broch, he could see Sophia on the roof, whirling round and looking quite wild. He worried about her, cared about her. He hurried past the meeting room and up the staircase that led to the roof.

'Flynn!'

'I'm here, mistress,' said Flynn, slightly out of breath. 'What can I do for you?'

'Nothing,' replied Sophia, turning to scrutinise him. She scanned his face and body and noted that he was out of breath. 'Have you been running?'

Flynn bowed deeply, allowing him to take a long breath to ease the stitch in his side.

'I was outside when I heard you call. I ran to be here by your side.'

Sophia nodded but still eyed him suspiciously.

'I need you, Flynn,' she said, and Flynn's heart leapt.

'Yes, mistress?'

'I want you to take our guest out of the jail and put her in the room next to mine. Make sure she has new clothes, food, and cleans herself up, understand?' Sophia inspected her claws as she talked, unaware of the blood draining from Flynn's face.

'But, why?' asked Flynn, unable to comprehend this turnaround in Sophia. She'd been all for killing the kitten when he left. The Order's plans lay on the assumption that Meissa would be in the broch's jail.

Sophia looked up from her claws, a quizzical look on her face. 'I didn't realise I had to justify myself to you, or anyone else, Flynn.' Her amber eyes flashed anger. 'But seeing as it's you, I'll tell you.' A smile began to play on her lips. 'I quite like this kitten, whatever she is called. We will train her up to become the next leader of the Ce, when I'm gone.' Her eyes met his and softened; her fur shone in the morning light. 'She will be our little warrior, Flynn.'

Flynn's heart leapt to his throat before tumbling to his stomach. He had so many deep, complicated feelings for this queen. He loved her with all his heart but at the same time he feared what she was capable of. She was the most strong-willed queen he had ever met. He had spent most of his life wanting to be with her, following her in the hope that one day she would show him that she felt the same way, but she never did. But now, now she wanted them to join together to teach Meissa; she had said "our little warrior". Sophia's voice brought him out of his daydream.

'Well? What are you waiting for? Go sort it.'

Giving a deep bow, Flynn turned and headed back down the stairs towards the jail.

Meissa woke with a start when she heard a key turn in the lock. The door squeaked open and a cat she hadn't seen before stepped into the room. Instinctively she tensed her body, waiting for the first kick or punch, then drew her breath in as her body flooded with pain. She could feel her blood starting to pump through her veins in an automatic fight or flight response.

Flynn felt nauseous at the sight of this little queen battered and beaten. She wouldn't meet his eye, and there was a large bloodied swelling on her cheek. What had Sophia done to her? He should have been here to stop it.

'Come with me,' he said, extending a paw and stepping towards Meissa.

She flinched backwards, a low growl emanating from her. If this cat was going to attack her, she would still fight, no matter how much it cost her.

'I'm not going to hurt you,' he said, hunkering down so he was almost level with her face. He put his paw under her chin and she flinched.

She looked into his eyes and saw kindness. They were sad eyes too, but kindness and love shone out from them. Meissa stretched out her good paw and let him help her to standing. The cat slid his arm gently round her middle to support her.

'I'm Flynn,' he said. 'I've come to help you, Meissa.'

They walked slowly up the stairs towards Sophia's rooms, Meissa limping and wincing with pain every step of the way. Flynn could feel her shaking and his heart went out to her.

'Where are you taking me?' Meissa asked in a tight, husky voice. She could barely speak through the pain.

'My mistress wants you taken to her rooms,' said Flynn. He felt her tense up. 'She likes you and wants to make you more comfortable.'

Meissa tried a laugh, but it came out more of a snort. 'Likes me? She did this to me!' Her voice disappeared into a squeak.

'I know, Meissa, and I'm so sorry for what Sophia did to you.' Flynn turned to face her. 'I'm truly sorry, but it won't happen again, I promise you that. She wants to train you, to become a warrior like her.'

Meissa stopped and looked at Flynn. He seemed to be genuine enough, but her torturer wanted to mentor her? She decided it was best to agree to whatever that mad queen wanted right now, at least it would keep her from harm for the time being. She would bide her time, her chance to escape would come.

They limped on down a corridor in silence, before Flynn stopped at a heavy wooden door. He leant across her and gave the door a push. It opened into a light and airy room, with a large wooden bed at its centre, and a roaring fire with the deepest, shaggiest fur rug Meissa had ever seen on the floor in front of it. On a dressing table to the side, sat a bowl of water and some cloths. Flynn tenderly settled Meissa on the bed then went over to the dressing table and returned with the bowl and cloths. The poor thing, he thought, as he handed her the wrung-out cloth. She placed it gently to her cheek and tried to ease the dried blood from her fur. Her lilac fur became pink as she wiped the diluted blood from her face and paws. Handing Flynn the cloth, she met his eyes.

'Thank you for your kindness.'

Flynn smiled at her, but the lump in his throat prevented him from speaking. Meissa eased herself further onto the bed and lay back on the pillows. They felt like heaven after her cold floor and rough blanket. Flynn pulled a soft cover over her.

'Close your eyes for a while, and I'll have one of the servants bring you up some food and new clothing,' he said, stroking her ears. She could feel a purr starting in her throat; she was so grateful for his kindness. She nodded, closed her eyes and within seconds was lost in a wonderful dream world without pain and suffering.

Sophia lay back and stared at the heavy grey clouds as they rolled over her head. A mist had come in and was soaking her fur, making it glint in the gloom of the afternoon. She had instructed one of her warriors to teach Meissa how to fight in claw-to-claw combat. She should have been downstairs to watch her protégée but craved the peacefulness that lying here on the roof brought her. She closed her eyes and felt her head swim with the sting of tiredness; she hadn't slept properly for weeks. Lying there, feeling the droplets of mist on her face, she heard a noise behind her.

'Don't stand there, Flynn. Come and sit beside me.'

Flynn approached and sat beside her. Sophia opened her eyes and smiled at him.

'Flynn, my Flynn,' she said, and Flynn's heart made a little leap. 'What woes do you bring to me now?'

Flynn shook his head, and putting a paw gently on her forehead, stroked between her ears. Sophia began to purr instinctively.

'I just wanted to make sure you were well. I worry about you, Sophia. We have known each other for so many years and I have never seen you like this before. You seem so troubled these days. It's not good for your soul.'

Tears welled in Sophia's eyes and gently rolled down her face. 'I miss him so much. I try to be a strong leader, but sometimes, sometimes I just want my father back.' Sophia turned and put her head onto Flynn's lap, and he cradled her there, feeling a purr begin in his chest.

Suddenly she wiped the tears from her eyes and sat up, breaking his hold on her.

'I need to get a grip. I can't let the rest of them see me like this.'

'You look fine,' said Flynn, wiping the water droplets from her face. 'So beautiful.' He smiled at her and the smile she returned was warm and gentle, reminiscent of the kitten she had once been.

The moment was broken by the entry of a cat stumbling onto the roof. They both bolted upright in surprise. The cat regained his footing and saluted both of them.

'Mistress, the prisoner has knocked out Greer. She is currently being held down by a couple of the cats but is doing her best to fight them off too. What do you want us to do with her?'

Sophia started laughing. 'I knew she was worthy of the Ce. Well, let her fight herself to exhaustion, but tell them to be careful and not fight back too hard, or they'll have me to deal with. Understood?'

The cat nodded, then turned and stumbled his way back down the stairs.

'I think we should go down and see what the little firecracker's up to, don't you, Flynn?' she said, turning to the stairs.

Flynn nodded and, as always, the obedient servant to his mistress, followed her.

Tom woke with a start. He had been dreaming of Meissa; she was running towards him smiling, her paws extended. In his dream she was enveloped in his arms, and he was breathing in the sweet smell of her fur...when he heard gruff male voices. His eyes shot open and he held his breath. Lying stock-still, he moved his eyes to try and see who was nearby. By slightly moving his head, he managed to see Zachariah who was lying not three yards away, wild eyes staring back at him. Zachariah flicked his eyes upwards, and following where he looked, Tom could see two cats in the next patch of heather talking to each other. He heard the words "prisoner" and "roughed up" and was straining to hear better when he became aware of movement beside him. Turning to look up, he glimpsed one of the biggest ginger cats he had seen since the orphanage, pass by him, only missing him by a few inches. As he walked, he stepped on Tom's tail and Tom winced but kept quiet, so he wouldn't give their hiding place away. The ginger cat hailed his companions by shouting and holding up some dead rabbits in the air to show them. The other two waved back and within a couple of minutes the big cat had joined them and the three of them had left Tom and Zachariah behind and were making their way to the broch.

At last Tom let out a sigh, not realising he had been holding his breath, and moved, stretching his muscles and giving his rather trampled tail a good rub. It responded with a sharp jab of pain.

Zachariah crawled through the undergrowth and joined him.

'That was too close,' he whispered.

Tom nodded. 'Why are you whispering?' he whispered back.

'In case they hear us,' Zachariah replied, nodding his head in the direction of the retreating figures.

As the cats were now at least a quarter of a mile away from them and engaged in raucous laughter, Tom doubted they would even notice them if they danced naked behind them, but he knew what Zachariah meant.

'Where's Felix?' he whispered.

Zachariah shook his head. 'I don't know. I only woke up a couple of minutes before you did, when I heard their voices.'

Tom looked up at the sky, dark clouds and mist obscured the sun but it had to be late afternoon. The day had been a long one so far and they still had several hours before they could put the plan Flynn and Felix had devised into action. He hoped Felix hadn't been captured whilst they had slept. He would never forgive himself if something happened to him.

'Might as well go back to sleep,' said Zachariah, tucking his paws between his legs and closing his eyes.

Tom could tell that within minutes he was sound asleep, his breathing was deep and a slow steady rhythm, but it was his twitching whiskers that gave the game away.

Tom lay there for a while looking up at the sky, watching the clouds grow darker before turning a violent pink as night grew nearer. Where was Felix? He thought to himself, surely he wouldn't have gone off on his own to do something, would he?

The air around him grew colder as darkness approached. Tom curled himself into a ball trying to keep warm, the sweet smell of the heather relaxing him. Taking a long slow blink, he felt his head droop to the side. He tried to keep his eyes open but each time he managed to open them they seemed to close themselves of their own accord; each time the blink becoming longer and longer. Eventually he fell into a deep sleep and into the dream world of warriors fighting and his Meissa waiting for him.

When he woke again, Felix was sitting beside him.

It was pitch-black, and Tom only knew it was Felix because of his familiar smell and the warmth emanating from his fur. He was looking towards the broch, his face in profile.

'Felix,' Tom whispered, 'what time is it?' As soon as he had said it, he realised the foolishness of his question. They had left all their personal possessions back in Edinburgh.

Felix looked down at him and smiled. 'It's killing time, little one.'

Tom's heart did a flip then sank without trace in his stomach. For all this time it had seemed like a big adventure, but now the three of them were going to have to raid a heavily fortified broch full of armed warrior cats. It seemed like the height of stupidity, a death wish if he had ever heard one. He took a deep breath and swallowed. This was for Meissa, that's all he had to keep in mind. It was for the cat he loved.

'Are you both ready?' whispered Felix.

Tom was aware of a movement beside him and assumed it was Zachariah making a move.

'I think I need to make a privy stop first,' Tom said, suddenly aware that he hadn't been to the toilet all day.

'A what?' Felix asked, before realising what he meant, and nodding.

'Don't want you to wee yourself in front of the Ce, do we?' he said, and Tom could hear him and Zachariah laughing as he walked a short distance away and relieved himself.

'Ready now, warrior?' Felix asked, as Tom returned. He nodded, glad the pair of them couldn't see him turning red under the moonless night sky.

The three of them crept slowly towards the threatening hulk of the broch, trying to make the tread of their paws as light as possible. The plan was simple enough. Flynn would drug the lookout cat's milk with a sedative, and then he would let down a rope for them to climb to the rooftop. From there it was only a short distance to the jail, and Meissa. Then it was back onto the roof and away before anyone realised what had happened. Flynn wouldn't be involved in order to keep his identity and safety intact.

So far, so good. They reached the base of the broch and as planned there was a rope dangling from the roof. Felix went first, climbing quickly, and with an agility Tom wouldn't have expected from a cat his size. Tom followed next, his arms and paws aching by the time he reached the top of the rope, then he was quickly followed by Zachariah. Once all three of them were on the roof, they pulled the rope up and hid it in the shadows before making their way to a staircase leading down into the building. As Tom climbed down from the piercing cold of the roof, warmth and light travelled up from below. The walls were lit by sconces and their light burned in his eyes as he crept past them. Ahead of them, Felix indicated that he was at the jail. They edged nearer to the heavy wooden door, aware of the dull sounds of cats below them. Felix peered through the peephole, then turned to them and shook his head. Tom's heart did another flip. Had they killed her? He nearly wailed, but Felix slapped a paw across his mouth to prevent him from opening it.

'She's gone,' he whispered into his ear. 'I'm going to find Flynn. Both of you stay here and stay hidden no matter what. Sophia will kill us on sight. Okay?'

Tom nodded, Felix's paw still covering his mouth, and then he was gone. Zachariah made a move to follow him, but Tom put out his paw and stopped him. He pulled him towards a darkened recess and crouched down so they were less likely to be seen, before whispering to him what had happened.

'We have to go and find her,' Zachariah half-mouthed, half-whispered.

Tom shook his head, drawing a claw across his throat to indicate that the cats would kill them if they were found out. Zachariah resignedly shrugged his shoulders and slumped down beside him.

It seemed like an eternity before the familiar outline of Felix's bulk slid in beside them in the recess. He shook his head and put his paw on Tom's shoulder.

'They've moved her to the room next to Sophia's,' he said. 'She's put a guard on the outside. There's no way we can get to her.'

'We can't leave her here with them!' cried Tom, his voice rising into a hoarse whisper. 'They'll kill her!'

Tom made to make a move and Felix pulled him back down.

'No!' exclaimed Tom. 'I'm going after her.'

He pulled away from Felix and ran down the corridor. Coming to a staircase, he paused for a moment before taking the steps up two at a time. By the time he reached the top, he could hear pawsteps below him. Hoping they were Felix and Zachariah following him, he paused to get his bearings. He heard Felix's voice telling him to follow the passageway round and then to wait for them. He turned, expecting to see Felix, but he was still coming up the stairs. Tom crept along the passage and could see the figure of a large, muscled cat standing outside a solid door, leaning on a heavy wooden staff. Tom stopped and kept in the darkness, so the cat wouldn't see him. The cat glanced around as though he could sense Tom was there but then went back to leaning on his staff. Felix and Zachariah came to a stop beside him and the three of them stood, motionless, watching the guard.

'Remember our lessons, little one?' whispered Felix into Tom's ear.

Tom nodded but thought to himself that he didn't remember any of it at all. His mind was blank, and his tongue was stuck to the roof of his mouth. He briefly saw Felix raise his paw and then all the sconces in the corridor went out. He could hear a brief scuffle then the light from the room lit the corridor briefly as Felix opened the door, dragging the body of the unconscious guard with him. Tom and Zachariah followed him in.

The room was large and comfortably furnished. On a dressing table sat a bowl of pink water and some cloths, and a warming fire burned in the fireplace. There was no sign of Meissa in the room although he could smell the sweet candy smell of her fur.

'She's been here,' Tom said, and Felix nodded.

Zachariah sat with a thud on the bed. 'What now? Do we hunt through the broch to find her?'

Felix shook his head. 'We wait.'

Tom sat down on the bed and put his head in his paws. This wasn't quite how he imagined rescuing Meissa in all those daydreams. And who knew if she would even come back to the room tonight. They could be sitting here until Sophia and her warriors came in and threw them all in the jail. Tom could feel his heart beating in his chest. Zachariah gave him a friendly punch on the shoulder. Felix paced the room, every now and again glancing out the window although what he was looking for, Tom wasn't sure. Just at that moment Tom heard pawsteps coming along the corridor. The pawsteps stopped, and the wooden floor outside the room creaked. Suddenly, they were all on high alert. Felix stood behind the door and waved his paw. The room was plunged into darkness. Meissa's form was briefly silhouetted in the corridor before it disappeared, and all was still and silent.

The next minute a flurry of movement swirled all around Tom. He tried tuning into his third eye, but he was distracted and couldn't focus properly on it. The next minute he was hit in the face by what felt like a lead weight before all the movement stopped, and his mind hovered in pitch-black silence. He came around after what seemed an age, although it must have only been a few minutes. He opened his eyes and looked up to see Meissa's bright green eyes looking back at him. She had her paws round him, holding onto him.

'Hello,' Tom said, smiling at her.

'I am so sorry, Tom,' she said. 'I didn't mean to knock you out. I didn't realise it was you.' Her eyes started to glisten, and Tom just lay there and stared into them, smiling.

Felix came into focus beside Meissa. 'Let's go – you can do the lovey-dovey stuff when we're not going to get killed.'

Outside, the corridor was as dark and silent as it

had been when they entered. Felix glanced both ways, then following in a single line, they crept through the passageway, back along the way they had come and up onto the roof. The cold air chilled them as they ran over to where they had left the rope. Throwing it over the edge of the roof they descended one by one. First Tom, who acted as lookout at the bottom, then Meissa. Zachariah followed quickly behind and finally Felix. When they had all reached the bottom, Felix let out a long, low whistle and as they ran off towards the loch, Tom heard the rope fall with a thud behind them onto the ground. As they reached the boat, Tom glanced back at the broch. He felt a surge of pride rush through him at what they had just achieved. His paws prickled and he could feel energy tingling within him. He glanced down at his pads; they seemed to be glowing. Tom shut his eyes then looked again. They looked completely normal. Had he imagined it? Felix beckoned to him and held out his paw to Tom. He put his paw in Felix's and without a backward glance, Tom jumped on board.

In the broch, Sophia was standing in Meissa's room, Flynn by her side. The guard had been taken away for questioning.

'Well, well, well. It seems our little warrior has been taken, Flynn.' She sniffed the air, her nose twitching. 'An old flame of mine, a smell I don't know, and one that feels familiar, but it can't be...no I'm mistaken,' she said, walking to the window and gazing out into the darkness. 'Someone must have helped them, Flynn, and when I find out who it is they will pay with their life.'

ELEVEN

Tom lay on the deck of the little boat looking up at the clouds as they tumbled past in the stormy sky. Feeling sick he pulled himself up, stumbling towards the side of the boat just as the boat lurched, plunging him off the deck and into the icy black waters of the North Sea. He briefly heard Zachariah scream for Felix, before a wave covered his head and he began to sink. Tom could feel himself sinking deeper and deeper. He started to flail his paws about hopelessly in a vain attempt at swimming. Just as suddenly as he had gone into the water, he was hoisted out of it and back onto the deck of the boat. Felix landed with a thump beside him. In between panting breaths, Felix tried to shout at him, but thankfully he just didn't have the energy and ended up slumping beside Tom, shaking his head.

'What did you think you were doing?' shouted Zachariah, taking over where Felix had left off. 'We could have all drowned!'

Felix let out a deep booming laugh from beside Tom.

'What are you laughing at?' exclaimed Zachariah.

'"All drowned"? I don't see you lying on deck, soaked to the skin and looking like a drowned rat, my princely one.' Felix laughed again.

Zachariah looked suitably abashed. 'Sorry, Felix, you know what I meant.'

'What were you thinking of?' said Felix, addressing Tom. He sat up, leaning back on his paws. His face looked like it was carved from stone, his fur sleek, shining in the darkness.

'I tripped,' Tom mumbled.

'"Tripped?" repeated Felix, 'You really are having a bad day, Tom.' He laughed, ruffling the fur on Tom's head.

Tom's eyebrows shot upwards and a dribble of seawater ran between them, down his nose and into his whiskers. He shook his head.

'A bad day? A bad life more like. You'd all be better off if I wasn't here,' Tom said.

Felix placed a wet paw on his shoulder.

'You're being silly little one. You have cats who love

you. This world is a better place because you're in it, never forget that.'

'I think the Cait of Ce would prefer it if I wasn't in it,' Tom replied, 'especially Sophia.'

'Enough, Tom.' Felix said, holding up his paw. 'We've been through this. We've got Meissa back, that's who you should be thinking about right now.'

That seemed to be the end of the conversation as far as Felix was concerned so Tom shut his mouth and tried to stop the tears of frustration brimming in his eyes.

Meissa stuck her head out of the cabin door, 'Come inside you lot, honestly, what are you like!' she said, shaking her head.

They retreated inside to the warmth of the cabin and spent the rest of the journey huddled in rough blankets, trying to get warm and stopping their teeth from chattering.

It was morning by the time the boat pulled into Leith docks and they headed their way back home. As they walked towards the New Town, Tom made his mind up: he wouldn't have his friends put themselves in danger and risk their lives for him. He would confront the Ce and Sophia himself and bring this whole sorry mess to an end.

Agatha opened the door for them when they reached Claudia's and although she gave a quick glance up and down, taking in their bedraggled appearance, she let them in. As soon as they entered the hallway, they were greeted by Claudia, running down the staircase.

'Where is she? Are you all okay? Where's Felix? Where's Meissa?' Her questions all came out as one long sentence.

Tom peeled himself out of his still sodden jacket and handed it to Agatha.

'Felix is fine. We're all fine,' he said as Claudia rushed past him and hugged a bruised and battered Meissa.

'Oh my, look at you. Is this what Sophia did to you?' Claudia cried, gently running a paw over Meissa's swollen face.

'Flynn?' Claudia asked, still looking at Meissa.

Zachariah shook his head. 'Don't know, never seen him. You'd better ask Felix about that one.'

Tom could sense the tightness in her voice. Surely, she didn't blame Flynn for what had happened to Meissa?

'Oh,' said Claudia, but left it at that. She turned to Tom. 'You look terrible. Why don't you go and have a bath and rest? You'll feel better after a rest.' She rang the bell and Agatha appeared.

'Run the kitten's baths, Agatha, and then warm their beds with hot water bottles.'

'Baths?' replied Agatha, as though it were the strangest thing in the world to hear of a cat bathing.

'Yes, Agatha, baths. I think drastic action is required, don't you?' Claudia waved a petite paw in Tom and Zachariah's direction. 'Those mats and tangles won't come out with just grooming, you know – and while you're at it, call Tarquair. Tell him he may be required here for some time.' She looked down at Meissa. 'And the vet, Agatha. We need the vet here as soon as possible.'

Agatha bowed and left the room. Claudia looked at Tom and Zachariah with a mixture of distaste and relief.

'Go – get clean and sleep,' she said, waving them away with a paw. She was still hugging Meissa tightly to her chest.

Needing no second bidding, they hastily retreated from the room and made for the stairs. Tom caught his reflection in a mirror as he passed. His fur was matted, dulled with saltwater and had a slight kink to it. Furthermore, he smelt of seaweed with just a hint of fish. Yes, he thought, Tarquair would indeed have his work cut out for him this afternoon.

Tom had just emerged from the bathroom in a cloud of steam when there was a soft knock on the sitting-room door. Zachariah, who was seated in front of a roaring fire, wrapped in his robe, shouted, 'Enter!' When the door opened, Tarquair stood there in all his silver glory. The markings of his moustache were even more pronounced than usual.

'Seawater is terrible for the fur, terrible!' he said with a flourish, bouncing into the room. He went over to Zachariah, who wasn't looking his usual dapper self, lifted his paw and examined his claws.

'Tut-tut, these will need surgery!' he cried, as Zachariah pulled his paw away rapidly.

Tom snorted with laughter but promptly stopped when Tarquair turned his attention to him. He still hadn't forgotten the humiliation of being defleaed by him the last time they had met.

'Master Thomas,' Tarquair said to him, bending low, 'you have learnt many lessons since we last met. I believe you are under Master Felix's tutelage. He will teach you well.'

'Er... Thank you, Tarquair,' Tom said, trying to hide his embarrassment. 'It's good to see you again too. I think you've got your work cut out with the pair of us this afternoon. We've been in wars of our own making, I'm afraid.'

Tarquair nodded sagely then he went to his doctor's bag and pulled out all manner of lotions, potions and what looked like instruments of torture. Tom insisted that he begin with Zachariah, who was only too happy to lie back and let Tarquair busy himself around him as he sat by the fire, half-dozing. However, before long it was Tom's turn under the brushes and combs, and as Tarquair

144

fussed with his unruly fur once more, Tom tuned out his mutterings and focused on the one thing occupying his mind: Sophia and the Ce lair. Tarquair finished at last and once more Tom stood at the mirror staring back at an Edinburgh dandy of a cat, almost unrecognisable from the bedraggled moggy who had been hauled back into that boat less than twelve hours previously.

'Thank you, Tarquair,' he said, shaking his paw.

Zachariah was completely asleep by the fire now, his face against the back of the chair, the careful styling of his fur mashed already. Tom glanced over at him. 'I apologise for Zachariah, but it's been quite a long day for us both,' he said, by way of an excuse.

'It does not matter,' Tarquair replied. 'I am here to do your bidding.' Pulling out a silver pocket watch, he checked the time. 'I must hurry.'

He packed his things back into his bag and started towards the door.

'Your mother must have been such a beautiful queen,' Tarquair said, shaking Tom's newly manicured paw.

'My mother?'

Tarquair nodded. 'She must have been beautiful, to have a kitten as striking as you. Have you never wondered about her?'

'Not really,' Tom lied, he had thought of little else since leaving the orphanage.

'Well, farewell master Thomas, I must make haste,' replied Tarquair.

He wished Tom well, shaking his paw again and disappeared down the stairs and out of the house.

Tom rushed back to his bedroom and pulled out the little case he had brought with him when he first arrived. He laid it on the bed and opened it, rummaging through the things he had discarded the moment he had come to live with Claudia and Zachariah. He found the locket he was looking for and opened it to reveal the tiny picture inside. The cat in the photo was indeed beautiful, but Tom had never known whether she truly was his mother or not. Her eyes were a similar colour to his, but her fur was the palest flaxen cream and her features were more refined and regal-looking than his general ginger ordinariness. He had always assumed this was his mother, but in reality it could have been any cat. His mother might even have stolen the trinket from another cat – Tom had no way of telling. But in his heart he knew that this really was his mother.

It was evening, and their rooms were dark when Zachariah woke with a start. Tom had sat there beside him as he snored and grunted, with his mother's locket in his hand. He felt so close to her, but he still ached for her love. He would never know it, never have that familiarity that comes with parents and siblings. He watched Zachariah as he twitched and meowed his way through dream fights and wars and had to smile at his paws twitching as though locked in combat. But this cat whom he had looked after during his kittenhood, and who now took care of him, would never be his true sibling, no matter how much Tom desired it; just as his mother would never hold him in her arms. She was dead and gone and nothing he could do would change that.

Agatha woke Zachariah with a knock at the door. As she entered, he let out a loud snort, and she stepped back in fright.

'It's all right, Agatha, it's just Zachariah fighting dragonflies in his sleep,' Tom laughed.

Agatha gave a wan smile and curtseyed but kept her distance.

'Mistress Claudia says dinner is ready and that Mr De'Ath is here to see you both.' She backed out of the room.

'Good girl, Claudia, perfect timing as usual,' yawned Zachariah, fashioning the fur on his head from mashed mess into a perfect fin with a couple of licks and a deft paw movement. He got up from the seat and stretched his full length, letting out a low moan as he did so.

'Aaaah, that feels better,' he said, grabbing a tailcoat

and turning for the door. 'Come on, Tom. Can't keep Claudia and Felix waiting.'

Tom pocketed the locket, picked up his tailcoat from the back of the door, and he and Zachariah walked down the stairs together. When they entered the dining room the candles had been lit and were throwing the shards of light around the room.

'Sparkles! Go get 'em, Tibbles!' laughed Zachariah. Tom just shook his head in despair at him.

Felix and Claudia were seated at one end of the table deep in conversation. When Tom and Zachariah entered, they both looked up briefly, then returned to finish their talk.

'Good evening, my little ones. Are you feeling more rested?' Felix now asked.

They both nodded, although Tom had had no rest, and in fact felt dead on his paws. He was not about to tell Felix that.

'Where's Meissa?' asked Tom.

'Sleeping, Tom,' replied Claudia. 'In fact Felix and I have been talking. It's not safe for any of you here, right now. He thinks it would be a good idea if you went away for a bit, out of Edinburgh, just till things calm down.'

Both Tom and Zachariah stood up and started to protest, but Felix raised his paw to silence them.

'It has already been discussed and decided. You will

stay at a friend's house until it's safe for you to return.' He looked over at Claudia, who looked down at her empty plate as though waiting for her food to appear.

'Claudia,' Tom said, 'you told us how we were to be strong and fight the Ce. How can we do that when we will be sitting at home twiddling our paws? And Felix, what was the use of all that training if you aren't going to let us fight? You know, moving objects by thought alone doesn't have much use if we are somewhere safe. Let us fight, that's what you've trained us for. And if we die for the cause, then so be it, but at least give us the chance.'

'No.' It was Claudia who spoke. 'For once you will both do what Felix tells you. He knows what's best. Trust him on this.' She gave Felix a small smile. 'Now, I don't know about you, but I'm starving.' She rang a bell and almost immediately Agatha appeared with their starters of smoked mackerel pâté.

Dinner was a subdued affair, with little chat, and afterwards Felix and Claudia removed themselves to the library, leaving Zachariah and Tom still sitting at the dining table.

'What now?' Zachariah asked, twirling his fork through his pads.

'I don't care what Felix says. He trained us to fight the Cait of Ce, and that's what I intend to do.' Tom had never felt so determined in his life.

'Maybe Felix and Claudia are right, I mean look at what they did to Meissa!'

'That's exactly why we should be fighting them Zachariah, so they can't do that to any other cat. It's me they are after. I'm the reason they tortured and killed those cats. I should be the one that hunts Sophia down. Have it out with her, cat to cat.' Tom thumped his paw on the table. 'Are you going to be a help or a hindrance to me, Zachariah?'

'Oh, bloody hell,' Zachariah said, rubbing his fur on his head into a mess again. 'Chances are I'll be more of a hindrance, but I guess you're stuck with me either way.'

Tom slept soundly that night, a deep dreamless sleep, and when he woke the next morning he felt full of energy and vigour for the day ahead. Zachariah, as usual, wasn't at his best in the morning, and it took ten minutes and the threat of a cold bucket of water to raise him from his slumbers.

'We need to take the fight to the Ce,' Tom said, as they sat at their breakfast of kippers and scrambled eggs. Zachariah just nodded and carried on eating.

'They're not going to expect that. We need a plan.' Tom picked at his kipper, trying to eat around the bones.

Claudia had walked into the room and was standing behind him in the doorway.

'I can't force you to stay, Tom, but I'm asking you

to think carefully before you do anything silly. Sophia has a dark heart, despite what Felix thinks, and she will kill you. Please don't do this.'

She had tears in her eyes and she turned away from them and wiped them, before regaining her composure.

'Thank you, Claudia,' Tom said, going to her and taking her paw in his. 'You know, you have been more of a mother to me in these last few months than I have ever known in my whole life. Thank you for caring for this unwanted kitten.'

At his last words, Claudia burst into sobs and ran from the room. Tom turned to Zachariah in astonishment.

'I was trying to make her feel better,' he said, totally puzzled by her reaction.

'Queens!' was all Zachariah said, as he wiped his plate clean and rubbed his belly in appreciation.

Tom sat back down at his seat and tucked into his kippers. He needed to keep his strength up if they were going after Sophia. All the time he was eating, his head whizzed with scenarios and options. The last time they had gone by steamboat to the broch but as he didn't know anyone who owned a boat they could hire he dismissed that option. As he watched Zachariah read the paper, he listed the alternatives in his head. A motor car was out – neither he nor Zachariah could drive and he didn't know where Felix garaged his one anyway. As for cycling, he thought, that might kill Zachariah even before they got out of Edinburgh. No, there was only one choice. They had to go by steam train and walk the remaining distance. It couldn't be that far, could it?

'Zachariah, put the paper down for a minute, will you? I need to sort out our travel plans. Do you know what time the trains are from Princes Street to Inverness?'

Zachariah looked up from his paper and a wrinkle appeared between his eyebrows.

'What do you think? Do I look like the kind of cat who has intimate knowledge of a train timetable?' He put a claw up. 'On second thoughts, don't answer that or you might be going on your own. Let's be daring and head up to the train station. You never know, there might even be a train leaving soon.'

'No need to be sarcastic,' Tom said, a bit hurt. 'I was just thinking out loud.'

'Oh, come on, huffy, surely we don't need to pack, do we? I just need to get Agatha to call and cancel my appointment at the tailors.'

Tom raised his eyebrows.

'What? A gentlecat can never have enough suits, you know. Then we can go on our big adventure, okay?' Zachariah eased himself out his chair and summoned Agatha with a ring of the bell.

He was as good as his word and as soon as he had

rearranged his tailor, and Tom had scribbled a note to Claudia telling her of their plans, they set off on their big adventure.

TWELVE

Their big adventure nearly ended at Princes Street train station when the arrivals and departures board stated that they had missed the one and only train to Inverness that day. Tom was trying to work out a criss-cross path of trains that would get them there, albeit by a circuitous route, when Zachariah whistled and waved him over to where he was standing beside a cat in uniform.

'I just thought I'd ask this fellow here,' he indicated with his paw the cat beside him, 'what the situation is with the trains, and how we get to Inverness without it taking a million years.'

'And?'

'And, he said the board is wrong and the Inverness train will be pulling into platform 3 in about fifteen minutes.'

'Zachariah, I could kiss you!' Tom cried, hugging him and birling him about.

'He means that in a purely platonic way,' Zachariah said to the station cat as Tom put him back down. The station cat smirked and sidled away from them.

'Great, let's get some tickets,' Tom said, walking off towards the ticket office.

'You do have money then? To pay for them?' enquired Zachariah, still standing on the concourse.

'Oh!' Tom said, with the horrible realisation that he had no money full stop to pay for train tickets, never mind money on him.

'Just as well I got Agatha to sub me,' Zachariah said, walking past and tapping his trouser pocket.

'You got the maid to sub you?'

'Don't knock it. You don't have any money at all, remember?'

They purchased the tickets and made their way to platform 3 to await the train. Tom constantly fidgeted and checked the time again and again. It seemed to be the longest fifteen minutes ever endured by a cat.

In due course, thirteen minutes and forty-two seconds to be exact, the train arrived, and before the passengers had even alighted, Tom jumped on and walked through the carriages until he found empty seats tucked away in a corner for both of them. He sat in the window seat, Zachariah settled in beside him, and lounged back. The train pulled out of the station and by the first corner Zachariah was sound asleep, lulled by the rocking movement from the tracks.

Tom sat and watched as the train passed through the outskirts of town, past industry and housing, until it opened out into wild countryside and they came to the Firth of Forth. The train rick-racked over the newly built red iron rail bridge, the solid ground giving way to the water far below. Tom felt giddy and he had to fight the urge to throw himself out the carriage door and into the water. He leaned back into his seat and closed his eyes to avoid the feeling. The train steamed on into Fife, past little and large villages, and onward towards Inverness. He dozed for a while and woke once only to find himself and Zachariah spooning into each other like the kittens they used to be. Tom turned over and fell back asleep only to wake again disorientated by the fact they were travelling beside mountains. Realising the train was skirting the Cairngorms, he sat up and rubbed his face and whiskers, trying to energise himself. He decided to do a bit of grooming using the glass of the window as a mirror, before slumping back into staring out of the window for a while. About five minutes before the train pulled into Inverness station he felt movement beside him as Zachariah yawned and stretched himself out.

'Have I missed much?' Zachariah asked, rubbing his ears and head. 'I'm starving. Is it lunchtime yet?'

Tom smiled, 'do you ever think of anything other than your stomach? It's early afternoon so it's way past lunchtime I'm afraid.'

'Damn,' replied Zachariah, 'Are we there yet? Maybe we can buy something to eat in Inverness.'

Tom just shook his head at his friend. Food was the last thing on his mind right now.

They had left Edinburgh in the sunshine but arrived in Inverness in the fog. Coming out of the station, Tom tried to orientate himself to the direction he should be heading but, unable to see ten yards in front of him, he had to admit defeat and returned to the train station to buy a map of the area. Not surprisingly, a broch inhabited by an ancient cat clan wasn't signposted, but by finding the river they had travelled up previously, Tom managed a rough estimate.

'That's bloody miles,' said Zachariah, peering over his shoulder. 'That will take weeks to walk. Sophia will have died of old age by the time we reach it.'

Tom gave him his best withering glance and started to refold the map.

'I'm joking, Tom, but come on, that will take ages! How about we cadge a lift at least some of the way?'

Grudgingly, Tom acquiesced, and Zachariah went ahead to scout out possible lifts in the area. Almost immediately Tom heard a whistle, and when he looked around, Zachariah was standing chatting to a pretty elderly queen. Tom tried to stop himself giving the queen the once-over, but the way she was dressed was extraordinary. On her head was a leather flying cap, strapped tightly beneath her chin; a tailored plaid jacket with leather strappings, and a sea-green full skirt hitched up at the front showing tan breeches underneath, completed the look.

'Tom Angel, may I introduce Mistress Morven. She has very kindly offered us a lift as far as a wee place called Doll. It will take us part of the way to our grandmother's house.' He winked at Tom at an angle that Mistress Morven couldn't see.

'That's very kind of you. Can we repay you in some way?' Tom said, well aware that the only money they had was the little change left over from the one-way train tickets and map.

'Och, away with you. I'll be glad of the company,' she said putting her paw onto Zachariah's arm. 'You can keep me amused on a normally very tedious journey hame.'

They took Morven's bags from her and carried them to a very smart but quite old steam engine vehicle, parked in front of the station. It looked like it had been cobbled together with parts of other vehicles. Zachariah eased himself into the passenger seat beside Morven and Tom hoisted himself into the back with the bags.

'Belt up, boys, it can get a bit bumpy,' Morven said, sliding on a pair of goggles, turning the key and revving the engine.

Bumpy was the word for it. Tom spent the whole journey with one hand clasping the overhead hand rail and the other trying to keep himself upright whilst still holding onto the shopping bags. In the front meanwhile, Zachariah and Morven bumped along happily hee-hawing with laughter as Zachariah enthralled her with tales of his luck with the queens and his various exploits when his luck ran out. They had long left Inverness behind, and although the fog was even thicker out here in the wilderness, Morven drove along the one-track roads and dirt tracks with the blind faith of someone who has driven the same roads for many a year. After what seemed to Tom a lifetime of being bumped and bruised, Morven screeched the vehicle to a halt at a crossroads.

'This is where we part ways, I'm afraid,' she said, leaning over to take a piece of paper and a fountain pen. She quickly scribbled some information on it and handed it to Zachariah, who for once blushed.

'Dinnae be a stranger if you're up seeing your grandmother,' she said, patting him on the paw.

He leant over and gave her a quick kiss on the cheek and it was her turn to blush.

'Oh, you!' she said. 'You'll turn an old queen's head, so you will!' She started laughing again and with much thanks and waving they saw her disappear into the fog.

Tom looked around his surroundings and his heart sank. They were truly in the middle of nowhere and there was no way they could see any landmarks to point them in the right direction. He took the crumpled map out of his pocket and unfolded it carefully.

'This sign says Brora two miles this way,' said Zachariah's disembodied voice from through the fog.

'It's okay. I think I've got it. If we go overland in this direction it should only be a couple of miles ahead of us.' Tom pointed in what he hoped was the right direction.

They started walking into the short shrub and heather. Mountains disappeared then reappeared in the fog. This certainly looked familiar, but how many miles were there like this?

'You do realise that if we go in the wrong direction they won't find our bodies for months out here, maybe even years!' said Zachariah, turning his collar up on his jacket and trying to flatten his ears under his cap.

'Don't remind me!' Tom said, trying to make himself into a tight bundle as they walked.

Before long the fog had seeped through their

clothing and they were wet through. Having only dressed in city clothing that morning, they weren't clothed for this Cataibh chill and before long Tom could feel his teeth starting to chatter. It was such a miserable walk that they didn't speak, just put one paw in front of the other. Tom repeated to himself, it's just one pawstep at a time, just keep going, it's only one pawstep at a time. They took turns at walking in front, as it was exhausting having always to watch where their paws were going, so they wouldn't stumble and fall. After what felt like an eternity, a hazy sun started to break through the fog and it slowly began to lift. Shapes began to form, and as they stopped for a few minutes to rest, Tom tried to focus on the landscape.

He strained his eyes as far as he could see, and in the distance he thought he could just about make out a lumpy solid structure.

'Zachariah, is that what I think it is?' Tom said, trying to haul him up from where he'd wearily collapsed moments before, by his soaking wet jacket.

'Who knows? Depends if you're looking for a broch or not,' Zachariah said, squinting. 'But what the hell, let's aim for it.'

Tom kept his eyes firmly on the hazy outline and set off through the bracken. They continued their muddy march, again taking turnabout to take the lead. Far in the distance beyond the mountains, Tom could see the sun getting lower and lower, the sky still hazy from the earlier fog. As they got closer, the structure took form and Tom could see with excitement that it was indeed the broch, or at least a broch. He could hear a river flowing nearby and could feel his heartbeat rise with anticipation. Zachariah grabbed him by the arm and he turned quickly, thinking they were being attacked. He was bent over, rubbing his side with his paw.

'Stitch,' was all he said.

'Are you okay?' Tom asked, concerned, but also aware that he wanted to get as close to the broch as possible before night fell. 'Do you want to rest for a minute?'

Zachariah nodded and took deep breaths to try and dissipate the stitch in his side.

They sat there on the wet ground in silence, each lost in their own thoughts. Goodness alone knew how they were going to get into the broch, never mind find Sophia and then what, kill her? Tom hadn't really considered what they were doing. It seemed like a good plan, back in the safety of Edinburgh, but now, out here in the cold of Cataibh, Tom began to doubt he could be brave enough to follow it through. The longer they sat there, the lower the sun sank beneath the mountains. As they set off again, the cloud descended and before long the fog was swirling around them. As they approached the broch, Tom could feel his hackles rise and his tail start to fluff at the prospect of fighting the whole Ce clan and their leader. From the base, the huge drystone building was dark and imposing. As they got closer, Tom looked up at its height and shape. There was no way they were getting in over the roof like they did the last time without help.

In the shadow of the broch they slowly inched their way round the perimeter. Tom was puzzled as there seemed to be a distinct lack of guards. Silently, they slipped in through the entrance, which opened into portals in either side of the wall, and onward to a meeting room with sconces blazing in the wall and a huge blazing hearth in the centre. Tom didn't have a clue where to go next, but at least they were in.

Zachariah whispered in his ear and pointed to a set of stone stairs set into the cavity walls. Tom could feel Zachariah's breath quicken as he spoke, and he could almost hear his heart beating as quickly as his own. Tom nodded, and they made their way stealthily towards the stairs. With Tom leading the way, they slowly negotiated the steps, as silently as they could. As he paused momentarily, he felt compelled to look through an opening into a hall – and there, sitting on an ornate throne, positioned at the centre of a long top table, was a regal-looking cream cat. She looked relaxed and was following two cats who were play-fighting in the middle of the room. She must have felt Tom's eyes on her because she turned slowly in his direction with a searching look. Tom ducked quickly, pushing Zachariah down with him. He had the distinct feeling that he had seen the cream cat somewhere before but couldn't remember where. They stayed hunkered down until it became apparent they hadn't been seen. They then continued up the staircase to the landing where Meissa's room had been. Up on the higher floors it was deathly dark and quiet, and Tom intuitively turned to his senses to guide him. Although he could only sense him with his third eye, he could feel Zachariah behind him, repeating each step he had taken, every fibre in his body on high alert.

They stopped in front of an ornately carved door. Tom, having remembered that Felix had said that Meissa's room was next to Sophia's, turned to Zachariah and whispered, 'This must be Sophia's room. We'll go inside and wait for her. Then, then we can deal with her.' He couldn't bring himself to say the words, kill her.

Zachariah nodded.

He closed his eyes, feeling the energy pulsing through his body and he could see everything as clearly as though it were daylight. He slowly turned the handle of the door and opened it gently. The room was in complete darkness and although he could see using his sixth sense, as soon as he walked into the room, everything suddenly went pitch-black.

When Tom opened his eyes everything was still dark, except this time he could just about make out faces above his head. Suddenly, his whole body gave a lurch and everything from head to tail started to throb with pain.

'What happened?' he asked, rubbing an aching joint. Felix's face suddenly swam into view in front of him.

'Sorry about that, little one. We thought you were the Ce doing a check,' he said, holding out a paw to help Tom up.

Tom glanced down to see the hump of a body lying face down on the floor, out cold.

'Ce guard,' acknowledged Felix.

He heard a groan behind him and he was able to make out Zachariah getting helped to his feet by Jones. He didn't envy him being taken down by Jonesy – that would have been a sore one, he thought.

Meissa emerged out of the gloom behind Felix. Tom smiled at her and made to hug her, but she put her paw out, holding him at arm's length.

'I can't look at you,' she said, her ears flattened against her head and she began to growl. 'I can't believe you would be so stupid.'

Tom looked at her, perplexed as to what she meant. He glanced from Meissa to Felix, but he too looked angry.

'Did you actually believe you could come here and

take on Sophia and the Ce single-pawed? What were you thinking, the pair of you. Have I not taught you anything? As for you, Zachariah,' Felix turned his focus to Zachariah who flinched at Felix's glare, 'did you really think you were helping Tom by coming along with him? Oh, I could bang your heads together. I'm so angry with both of you!'

At that moment Tom heard a low whistle, almost like a birdsong, coming from the doorway and on turning his head, he saw Jones giving Felix a sign that someone was coming.

'We need to leave, now,' said Felix. 'I'll deal with both of you when we get home.'

He pushed Tom and Zachariah out the room and into the dark corridor. With Jones, Shepard and Meissa leading, they hurried along the hallway. Tom felt ashamed of himself. He hadn't thought that Felix and his friends would try to find them. He had wanted to make the situation better, but once again he had been left feeling like he was a silly little kitten who knew nothing. And now even Meissa was angry with him. The situation couldn't be any worse.

They had just come out onto the roof when Tom heard a voice from behind them, and he was pushed unceremoniously onto the ground by Shepard, who turned and drew himself up to his full, imposing height. He stood shoulder to shoulder with Jones as they shielded Meissa,

166

Tom and Zachariah with their bodies. Through their legs and tails Tom could see a queen standing at the entrance to the stairs. He recognised her as the cat in the central hall. She was the most strikingly beautiful cat Tom had ever seen; tall and graceful, with piercing amber eyes, and fur that sparkled in the moonlight. His muddled brain wouldn't let him recall where he thought he'd seen her face before. She seemed familiar, but he was sure he had never met her. Felix left the others and strode towards the queen, stopping a few feet in front of her.

'What a surprise seeing you here, Felix. Missing me were you?' she said, staring Felix in the eye. 'Please don't say you've forgotten me – that would be so sad. Remember, I used to be the love of your life.'

'Don't, not here. Let the others go. Take me as a prisoner if you want, but they have done you no harm,' Felix said.

Sophia took a step closer to Felix and was standing nose to nose with him, their whiskers almost touching. If someone had happened upon their little scene they would have looked like they were in love, instead of deadly enemies. Felix didn't flinch for a second, but Tom could tell that Shepard and Jones were gunning for a fight; he could feel their energy rise and see their tails starting to fluff up.

A low grumbling growl started from both Sophia

and Felix, and Sophia showed her teeth in a threatening manner.

'You never could handle a real queen, could you, Felix?' she said, her whiskers still gently touching his.

'And you could never control that temper of yours,' he replied.

She smiled and moved her head slightly to the side of his face, before leaning in and kissing him gently on the cheek. Sophia looked over to where Shepard and Jones were standing in front of Tom, Zachariah and Meissa.

'Is that my little warrior Meissa I see? Bring her to me. She's mine, Felix,' she whispered in his ear. 'I want her back, and you know I always get what I want.'

Tom could see Felix arch an eyebrow in defiance, as if to say to her, you think you can tell me what to do?

'Wouldn't you rather have an old flame back in your life instead of some troublesome kitten? I mean, I could be so much more useful to you than she ever will be, Sophia.'

'I'd much rather have Thomas Angel than you, Felix. No offence, but you're a bit long in the tooth now.'

Tom bit his lip, trying not to breathe so Sophia wouldn't notice him.

All the while Felix was talking, Tom could see him surreptitiously signal to Jones with his claws and Jones very slowly began to move Meissa, Tom and Zachariah away from Felix and Sophia.

'Get her back here now!' said Sophia, not taking her eyes off Felix. 'You want to play games, Felix? Well, you know how I like playing games. First of all, bring me my little warrior back here.' She signalled Jones to bring Meissa back to her. 'Now!'

Jones glanced at Felix, who nodded. Tom thought he saw him twitch his whiskers, but he couldn't be sure of it. Jones slowly walked to Sophia with his paw on Meissa's shoulder.

'It's okay. I can look after myself, Jonesy,' Meissa said, smiling up into the big cat's face. She went and stood beside Sophia, who put a protective arm around her.

Out of nowhere came a long loud shout of 'No!'

Tom spun round quickly to see Zachariah shoot past Felix and throw himself at Sophia. It was only then he realised she had a claw at Meissa's throat, its point sinking into her fur. Zachariah was mid-air when Sophia took her claw from Meissa's throat and shot it out in front of her towards him. Zachariah froze for a second and then with a slashing action using her claw, Sophia made Zachariah drop to the ground. Zachariah grabbed his arm, stemming the blood flowing from it. Tom ran to him, but Shepard caught him and threw him back against the outer wall, into the darkness. Now all hell broke loose. Three of the Ce warriors appeared on the roof, and Shepard and Jones battled with them. Sophia took hold of Meissa by the throat again and with the other paw was trying to hold back Felix as Meissa bit into Sophia's arm to let her go. Tom ran to Zachariah and helped him to his paws. He could see the blood running down his arm.

'Just a flesh wound. Looks worse than it feels,' Zachariah said, smiling but wincing with every movement he took. He turned to see Meissa running from Sophia and towards Felix. Sophia raised her arm like she had done with Zachariah and pointed her paw towards Meissa. Tom let go of Zachariah and ran, yowling from the pit of his stomach, towards them. He raised his paw and aimed it directly at Sophia. She turned to look at where the noise was coming from.

'Who the—?' was all she managed to say, before the energy strobing from his paw hit her and flung her back towards the staircase.

She landed with a thunk, her head against the stonework, which knocked her out cold.

Tom stared at his paw, unable to comprehend what had just happened. Meissa ran to him.

'That was amazing, Tom!' Meissa said, positively beaming at him. He gazed down into her beautiful green eyes and for a minute he heard or saw nothing else. Felix soon jolted him out of it by grabbing him by the arm and running him towards the edge of the roof.

'Where's Zachariah!' Tom yelled. He wasn't leaving without his best friend.

'Shepard's got him. Now jump!' Felix yelled, as he thrust both Meissa and Tom towards the precipice. Looking over the edge, Tom could only see darkness at the bottom, but he did as he was told, grabbing hold of Meissa's paw before launching themselves into the air. Tom landed with a thump on all four paws. He looked to Meissa who was standing upright brushing herself down.

Tom took Meissa's paw and ran as quickly as he could in the general direction of the loch. They caught up with Shepard who was weighed down, carrying Zachariah over his shoulder. Huffing and puffing, Shepard pointed the way to the boat and the three of them ran for their lives towards it.

The skipper already had the engine running, and as they approached the boat, he held out his paw to help them on board. Meissa went first, then Tom, who helped Zachariah on board. Last to board was Shepard who kept looking backward towards the broch.

It was eerily silent for several minutes, then came the sound of someone pounding through the undergrowth, cursing every now and again as he ran. Out of the darkness Jones charged and flung himself at the boat, landing with a thud on the deck.

'Go! Go! Go!' he shouted, and the skipper slammed the shaft to the floor and the boat shot off down the loch and into the river, the Ce warriors running in pursuit on the banks of the river.

'Where's Felix?' Shepard said to Jones. Jones shook his head.

'Sophia's got him.'

THIRTEEN

Flynn and Sophia stood side by side in the room facing Felix. He had been chained to the floor with a heavy metal collar round his neck.

'Not so brave now are you, Felix?' Sophia walked up to him and prodded him with the toe of her boot. 'How I could have ever loved you, I'll never know.' She hunkered down so she was at eye level with him. 'And now look at you - you're everything I despise in a cat. Weak. Old. Scared. Impotent. I loathe you with every bone in my body.' She turned away from him.

'You hate those things, Sophia, because that's what you're most scared of yourself! You're scared to show any weakness, scared that when you're older there will be no one to fight for you, to be loyal to you for no reason, and that's because you chose this poisoned chalice of power instead of love and family. Is that not what you loathe? I only remind you of what you could have had, what we once had. Before you threw it all away.'

Sophia turning, ran screaming at Felix, lashing out with her paws, clawing and kicking him anywhere she could reach.

'How dare you! How dare you speak to me like that! I... I...hate you, Felix!' She swung at him one last time with her claws drawn, then turned and ran from the room.

Flynn still stood by the doorway. Once Sophia had fled from the room, the silence closed in on them.

'Did you have to, Felix?' Flynn said calmly. 'Did you have to bite back at her? You know it's only words with her. She doesn't mean it. She is just lashing out at you.'

Felix wiped blood from a cut on his eye. 'She did that all right. She's getting worse, Flynn, much worse than you said. Can't you do something before she harms everyone around her as well as herself?'

Flynn leaned against the door jamb and shrugged. 'I don't know what to do, Felix. She's changed, and I don't know what to do about it. This thing about Tom, I mean, it's just totally irrational, but she's hell-bent on killing him. I mean, what's he ever done to her?'

Felix shook his head.

'Thank goodness she didn't realise he was with us

tonight. That was madness, the pair of them coming up here themselves. What was Claudia thinking, letting them go? I just don't know what's happening anymore. It's all mad, and I just don't know where it's going to stop. Once Sophia's got the bloodlust, it's never going to stop, is it?'

Flynn sighed and shook his head. 'I can't believe how she's changed, Felix, since Kasperi died.' He paused. 'It's tipped her over the edge. I mean, for years he had driven her harder and harder, to fight, to kill, to only focus on the Cait of Ce, nothing else mattered, and now, now she seems to have slipped over into madness. I don't know what she's going to be like from second to second, never mind day to day. I don't know what this insanity is about that's taken hold of her, no one does. She talks to no one now. She just goes around muttering to Kasperi. It's like she thinks he's still here. I just don't know where it's going to end. I just know it's going to end badly. For all of us.'

As Felix nodded, the collar round his neck caught him, and he coughed.

'I can't even help you. If she found out I did something like that she would kill me.'

'I'm fine – don't worry about me,' said Felix. 'I'm just worried about what she's going to do to those kittens without me there to protect them.'

'Claudia will look after them,' replied Flynn.

'If I hadn't listened to Claudia, they would have

been somewhere safe by now, not running around Cataibh on their own!' said Felix, the collar pulling on his throat again.

The pair of them descended into silence again and Felix heard footsteps approaching. They exchanged a glance, then Flynn straightened himself into a more forceful stance over Felix.

A guard entered the room.

'Pardon me, sir, but the mistress is calling for you,' he said. Then he added, 'She's quite anxious to see you.'

He bowed and backed out of the room.

'I had better go and see what she wants,' said Flynn, turning to the door.

'Good luck.'

Sophia's room was in darkness except for a single candle on the windowsill. She stood beside it, staring out into the darkness. Flynn entered the room but stayed standing just within it.

'Flynn, come here,' said Sophia, not turning to see whether it was him or not. She could tell him by his smell. 'Come hold me.' She reached out a paw into the darkness.

Flynn walked over to her and reached out to hold her paw in his. She turned, and putting her head on his shoulder, started to weep like she would never stop. Flynn hesitated for a moment then put his arms around her. Sobs racked her body. She was unable to breathe properly, her breath coming in gasps. She couldn't stop, and every time she thought she was starting to feel herself calm down, she would think of something and the painful heartache would come over her again and again. She cried for everyone she had ever loved and everyone she had ever lost – for Kasperi, for Felix, for every Ce warrior she had sent into battle who hadn't returned. Their ghosts all haunted her in one way or another, and tonight she felt like she was purging them, one tear at a time. A long while after the tears had started, she felt herself calming down. Her stomach hurt from the sobbing. Her throat was dry and her eyes puffy and sore from the salt in her tears. Flynn put a paw-pad under her chin and lifted her head from his shoulder. She could see it was wet from her tears.

'Do you want to tell me about it?' he asked quietly. 'This isn't just about Felix, or about that little kitten, Meissa. So what is it about, Sophia?'

She looked at him a long time before answering.

'I killed them, Flynn. I killed them all. I drowned them with my bare paws. And they haunt me. Every night, when I close my eyes I see them, I hear them mewling. I have to relive what I did to them every night of every month of every year. I hear them and I see them.'

'Who?'

As she looked at the ground, the silence stretched between them, but neither of them spoke.

'My own kittens. I was so angry that I kept my pregnancy a secret, and when they were born I killed them all.'

Flynn could hardly breathe. He wanted to say something but feared when he opened his mouth he would betray himself and tell Sophia what he knew.

'I've had to live with what I did for all these years. Only Kasperi knew the truth, and I knew he would never tell another living soul. But he's gone now, and every night they still haunt me but now I have no one to tell about them. I feel so alone.'

Flynn moved his paw to stroke her ear. She looked up at him.

'Do you know what it feels like, Flynn, when you have no one to talk to, no one to share your pain with? I'm in command of all these cats. I decide who lives and dies on a day to day basis, but not one of them loves me enough to care whether I live or die or what hell I go through every day for them. I gave my love to Felix and—' Sophia paused, the memory of what had happened still painful after so many years had passed. '—and he let me down. He went away with Claudia and left me.'

'That's not what happened, Sophia,' said Flynn gently. He just wanted to put his paws round her and tell her that he was there for her, but he knew she wouldn't believe him. 'You banished Felix and Claudia. What did you expect them to do? They had to leave, and after everything that had happened, no one wanted to know them when they left. They only had each other to rely on. You weren't around to see the fallout you had caused, but they were left with nothing. Perhaps less than nothing.'

Sophia looked up at Flynn and her eyes filled with tears again. She swallowed them back down.

'They made their choice, Flynn. I told Felix to give her up and I would forgive him, but he wouldn't. They both had to go.'

'What choice did you give him? He and Claudia had known each other since they were kittens. They were only ever friends – still are only friends. Is this what this is all about, Sophia? Trying to get back at your ex-love and his supposed mistress? Is this what all this fighting has been about? About Felix? And what about Thomas Angel? Where does he fit in to this picture? Why are you after him, so obsessed with hunting him down and killing him? What's he ever done to you, Sophia? What's his secret?'

Sophia looked Flynn directly in the eyes, her pain and anguish replaced by her usual steely determination.

'He's the one who got away.'

FOURTEEN

Tom sat on the deck of the boat, his head lolling over the side, trying not to be sick for the fourth time. He hadn't eaten all day and he was now retching with an empty stomach. Zachariah stuck his head out of the cabin.

'You coming in yet?' he asked, just as another wave of nausea swept over Tom and he launched his head in the direction of the choppy waters.

A cold sweat rose up from Tom's tail and travelled all the way through his body, and he knew it wasn't just the seasickness that was making him feel this way. What was Felix going through? Was he still alive? Tom felt like he had just been made an orphan all over again. He had lost the cat he felt was his only family, and he knew that the empty, hollow feeling in his heart and stomach wasn't just due to him being on this boat. He felt an overwhelming loss; he had just found Felix, and now he had lost him again. Worse still, it was Tom's fault that Felix had been in the broch. If he hadn't had the crazy idea that he could defeat Sophia then Felix would never have followed him there. The tears swelled in his eyes and he just wanted to scream out, to go back and kill everybody in that broch – make Sophia suffer like he was suffering. He wanted Felix back no matter what, whether Felix was dead or alive, he wanted him back with his friends. He lay his head on the edge of the deck and stared down into the water, his mind drifting through times past. He felt a paw stroke the back of his head gently, pulling his mind back to where he was. Meissa put her cheek against his.

'He's still here. Can't you feel him?' she whispered in his ear. 'Felix will never leave you as long as he's in your heart.' She placed a small, delicate kiss on Tom's cheek. He looked at her, the tears still rolling down his cheeks.

'We'll get him back, no matter what. We're going to bring Felix back to his friends, his family,' she said. The tears welled up in her eyes, and Tom put his arms round her and pulled her close. They sat there, the two of them weeping for more family lost than just Felix, for a very long time.

Eventually Shepard came out on deck, looking as sick as Tom was feeling.

'Come on you two, inside. Last thing we need is for you two to get sick. Claudia would kill me.'

Tom helped Meissa to her paws, then went back into the little cabin, which was stuffy and smelt of wet fur. Meissa sat down opposite Zachariah, between Jones and Tom, and took Tom's paw in hers.

'So, what's the plan for getting Felix back then?' she asked, looking over at Shepard who was standing near the doorway in case he needed a quick exit. 'We can't leave him with the Ce. Sophia is unstable. There's no knowing what she will do'. Her voice was now strong and determined; the softness of it when she had been talking to Tom was gone.

'Sophia and Felix were in love once. There's no way she'll hurt him,' replied Shepard. 'She still loves him.'

'Well, forgive me for saying, Shepard,' Meissa said, 'but that just shows what little you know of queens! That means she'll be even more volatile. There is nothing more evil than a queen scorned and all that. No, that means we'll have to be even quicker to move, before she flips out. What has she been like in the past? Does she ever show leniency? From the little time I've spent with her, I doubt it. She has a short temper. I know that only too well, and if she starts going off on one, well, there's no telling where it will lead.'

Tom squeezed Meissa's paw. He stared at this

amazing, determined, beautiful little queen and wanted to shout 'I'm in love with you', from the top of the boat's mast.

'What?' she said, giving him a quizzical look, but she gave his paw a little squeeze back under the table.

He heard the door slam back on its hinges and turned to see Shepard's tail disappear outside before hearing retching noises.

'God, what are you lot like!' said Meissa, half-laughing, half-exasperated. 'I think we'd better wait till dry land before we come up with a plan, don't you?' she said, smiling.

Tom said nothing but smiled back. He couldn't think of anything else in the world now he had the paw of the cat he loved in his.

By the time the boat docked in Leith, they were a sorry bunch. Tom and Shepard were still a bit green about the gills and no better once they were on dry land. Meissa, who was still carrying the scars and bruises from her time with the Ce, walked along the quayside by Jones and Zachariah. Jones was sporting the most spectacular purple swollen eye, and whilst Zachariah had managed to bandage his arm, the blood was seeping through the wrappings. Out on Commercial Street, Tom was surprised to see Ash sitting at the wheel of a sleek, dark green motor car. As he helped

Meissa into the front seat, Ash whispered to Tom, 'Felix?'

Tom shook his head and without another word climbed into the cramped back seat alongside Jones, Shepard and Zachariah. Nothing more was said on Felix's absence as they sped through the streets to Claudia's house.

As the car pulled up outside Claudia's, the door of the house was flung open and Claudia ran out into the street followed by a weeping Agatha. Opening the back door of the car, Claudia pulled Zachariah into a hug. Zachariah, who was trying to get out the car at the time without moving his bandaged arm, mewled in pain as Claudia grabbed him.

'Oh my, oh my! Are you okay? Let me look at you. You are okay, aren't you? Oh, look at your arm, oh my poor kitten!' Claudia alternatively hugged Zachariah close, then pushed him away to look at him, before grabbing him and pulling him tight again. 'You are banned from ever leaving this house again! Do you hear me?'

Whilst this exchange was going on, the rest of them managed to sneak out of the car and into the hallway of Claudia's house, followed by a still weeping Agatha. Tom felt bad that she had obviously been punished for helping them, but when he made a move to speak to her, she threw her hands up, started sobbing even louder and ran off in the direction of the kitchen.

Claudia came into the hallway, her arm still around

Zachariah. She was talking to him in a stern voice but all the while she lovingly stroked his fur.

Once they were all gathered in the hall, they stood about, unsure what to say. It was Claudia herself who broke the silence.

'I don't know what you pair were thinking!' she said. 'I don't know whether to slap you both or hug you! Thank goodness you're still alive. You don't know what that queen is capable of!'

She turned to Shepard, her paws on her hips. 'And as for you lot, you're no better than the kittens! What were you thinking getting them involved with the Order in the first place? Just because you've fought the Ce and survived doesn't mean the kittens would have. Seriously! And where's Felix? I bet he's sloped off home already, leaving you lot to clean up his mess as usual!' She finally stopped shouting, but only once she had realised that none of them had moved or said anything.

'Where's Felix?'

Shepard stepped forward and gently put his paw around Claudia's shoulders. He steered her into the library, whether to give her privacy or to save the rest of them the sight of her pain, Tom didn't know, but a few moments after they went into the room, a resounding yowl of 'No!' came echoing from it, and seemed to hang in the hallway where they stood.

Claudia came rushing out of the library, with Shepard following her. She ran up to Zachariah and grabbed both his paws.

'He's wrong. Tell me he's wrong!' she cried, barely able to breathe. Tom wanted to run to her, to take her pain away for her but he couldn't, no one could. Zachariah just stood stock-still, not saying or doing anything as Claudia gripped his arm and reopened his wound. The blood flowed freely, but none of them noticed it.

'He can't be gone. He can't,' Claudia said, her voice smaller. She was still holding onto Zachariah who stood there, not knowing what to do or how to comfort his aunt.

It was Meissa who took control of the situation. She walked over to the corded bell by the door and rang it. A puffy-eyed Agatha appeared after a few seconds.

'Agatha, I want you to call for the vet to come and see your mistress – she is quite distressed as you can see – then bring her some sweet cream up to her room. The vet will need to attend to Zachariah's arm as well, let him know he will have two patients. Once you have done that, can you see to it that Tom and Zachariah are given baths, and Shepard and Jonesy are given something to eat? Once I've settled Claudia, I'll wait for the vet in the library. Please send him to me when he arrives.'

Agatha nodded like it was the most natural thing in the world to have been given orders by this feisty little queen and disappeared through a doorway, no doubt to get straight on the telephone to the vet. Meissa then walked over to Zachariah, who was still standing stiff as a board, his aunt still hanging onto his arms, weeping onto his shoulder.

'Tom, give me a hand,' she said, gently touching Claudia on the small of her back and easing her paws away from Zachariah. Tom could hear Zachariah breathe a sigh of relief now that someone had taken control of the situation although he still looked shell-shocked as between them they gently helped Claudia up the stairs to her room.

Returning to the hallway, Tom could see everyone was still milling about, not knowing what to do with themselves. Agatha appeared from the dining room and curtseyed.

'There's food ready, sirs,' she said, obviously unsure whether to call it breakfast, brunch or lunch. She disappeared back into the room, followed by Zachariah, Jones and Shepard. Tom didn't have an appetite, so he walked wearily back up the stairs to his room to await his bath and try his best to avoid thinking of Felix.

Zachariah came into their rooms half an hour later. He had eaten, and Shepard and Jones had departed to their own homes. He was pressing a paw to his cut arm even though the blood had now dried again.

'How's Claudia?' Tom asked him.

Zachariah slumped into the easy chair opposite Tom and ruffled the fur on his head.

'The vet's with her now,' he said. He kicked off his boots and rubbed his pads. 'I don't think she's too good though, just by what Shepard and Jones were saying. There's a lot of history between her and Felix. I don't know what she'll do if that Sophia has killed him. I don't want to think about that, never mind Claudia, and we've only known him a few months.' Zachariah slumped back into the chair and stared in silence into the fire.

Tom watched the flames crackle and spit in the hearth and tried not to think about what would be happening to Felix. Whatever it was, he just hoped it was painless and quick, but he doubted it. It was true, they had only known Felix a few months, but he felt like he had known him all his life. He had so much to learn from him; there was no way he could be dead. Surely if this Sophia was the cat Felix had told him he had loved all those years ago, she wouldn't, couldn't, kill him. Surely you couldn't do that to someone you once had feelings for? Then again, he had seen them on the roof of the broch. There had been nothing but pure hatred pouring out of both of them. He couldn't imagine hating anyone that much, no matter what they had done to him. Then he thought about how he felt about Meissa, and how he had felt about Zachariah when he had seen the pair of them together. Yes, he thought, he could understand Sophia's single-minded hate and how it might unhinge her after all this time. Why did she want Meissa though, and why her obsession with killing him? What had he ever done to her? On the other hand, he thought, she had called Meissa her little warrior. How crazy was that cat?

Agatha entered the room with a knock and a curtsey.

'Sirs,' she said, 'Master Tom's bath is ready.' She curtseyed again then left the room.

'Two baths in the space of two weeks, Tom, that's not normal for a cat,' said Zachariah, shaking his head as Tom eased himself out of the seat with surprising stiffness.

Tom folded his clothes beside the bath although he doubted they would ever be in any fit state to be worn again. He eased himself into the hot, steaming water and sighed as the heat soaked his fur and seeped into his muscles. For once in his life he enjoyed lying in the water, just letting his thoughts drift, although this time it was not to Felix and the Cait of Ce, but to Meissa and himself on the deck of the boat.

Felix woke with a start and then realised he was still in the dark, dank cell in the broch. He could hear screaming in the distance and tried to ascertain where and whom it was coming from. He didn't know whether all the cats had escaped. When he had been dragged off the rooftop, he had left Jones running for the edge off the top. There was no way of knowing whether they had all got away safely. He made a note to himself to ask Flynn the next time he saw him. He turned over and was yanked back by the collar round his neck. He had forgotten he was wearing it, although goodness knows how. It weighed a ton and tightened every time he moved his head. He heard clanking at the door and keys turning in the lock. At the same time, his stomach gave a loud grumble. Must be food, he thought. He didn't know how long he had been there, but it must be the next day by now, which meant he had probably last eaten more than eighteen hours ago. He tried to sit up, and his body protested. He wasn't as young as he once was, and his muscles complained at the beating he had taken.

The door swung open, and Sophia was standing there beside a guard. She entered whilst the other cat remained at the door.

'Who were the kittens with you last night?' she said, standing over him.

Felix said nothing but looked past her at the other cat.

'I asked you who the kittens were, Felix. I expect an answer.'

'Is this Ce hospitality nowadays, Sophia? My, my, your standards have slipped since I was last here. I remember the feasts we used to have. Freshly caught salmon, cream from the village cows, rabbit and grouse – those were the days. These days it seems it's your habit to starve your prisoners, or am I just a special case?'

Sophia sighed and turned to the guard behind her.

'Go bring some food. Whatever is in the kitchens will do – anything to shut him up.'

The guard bowed to her and left them alone.

'You still haven't answered me, Felix. I'm waiting,' she said, walking closer to him and giving him a prod with her boot again. 'And I don't like to be kept waiting...'

'What was the question again?' said Felix, smiling as though they were exchanging pleasantries.

Sophia hunkered down in front of him until they were eye level to each other.

'Let me put it another way then, seeing as you seem to be incapable of answering that simple question. Was Thomas Angel with you last night?'

Felix paused before answering her. 'No.'

'You liar!' she screamed, yanking the chain attached to Felix's collar and pulling his face close to hers. 'I could smell him. It was too familiar a smell to be anyone else. It's the only explanation – what else could it be? Which one was he, Felix? Tell me. Which kitten was my son?'

FIFTEEN

Felix sat in stunned silence. The minutes stretched out like hours before he spoke.

'Your son?'

'Well, well, well, that surprised you, Felix De'Ath. What's the matter? Didn't think I was the maternal type?'

Sophia let go of the chain she was still holding in her paw. It clattered to the floor, but neither she nor Felix moved.

'Tom was brought up in an orphanage. He has no parents. You're wrong about him. You've got him mixed up with another kitten.'

'Really?'

'Yes, really,' replied Felix. He was rapidly trying to remember any morsel of information that might point to Tom being Sophia's kitten. It couldn't be true. How could it? Tom had said that he had a locket with a picture of a cat he assumed was his mother. If that was the case, why hadn't he recognised Sophia last night on the roof? It just couldn't be true! Except it could. What Felix found most disturbing was the thought that Sophia could have loved another cat enough to have his kitten, but then why put him in an orphanage? He saw she was watching him intently.

'Little brain ticking over with all the possibilities, Felix?' she said.

'Tom can't be your son. That's all there is to it,' he said, sounding surer than he felt.

'Why not?'

'Not even you would put your own kitten in an orphanage, Sophia – and now, trying to kill him. Why?'

Sophia sat down on the ground beside him. Her face softened into the cat Felix had fallen in love with all those years ago.

'Kasperi saved him. I drowned the rest of my own kittens.' She put up a paw to stop Felix from speaking 'I know, what an evil queen from hell. Well I am – get used to the idea. I only found out about him when Kasperi was dying – my dear, sweet, beautiful Kasperi. He thought he had done the right thing, hiding this kitten from me, but all I could see was a pretender to my throne. No one will take the Cait of Ce away from me.' She smiled to herself.

'You know, he smells the same sweet musky scent as my Kasperi. That's how I knew it must be him.'

'This is all about the Ce? You're going to kill an innocent kitten, so you can be king of the castle? Are you mad?'

'Queen of the broch actually, but yes, I've killed before. What's another little ginger kitten?'

'Another little ginger kitten? He's not just another ginger kitten, Sophia. He's your kitten! Your own flesh and blood! Surely, he means more to you than just another kitten to kill! For goodness sake, cat, have you no soul? Do you not care that you're talking about killing your own flesh and blood like you would kill a mouse for dinner?'

'So, I was right – he was the ginger one. Thank you for telling me that although I have to say I kind of hoped it was the black kitten. At least he had a little bit of go about him. The ginger one wasn't up to much, but then again that will make him easier to kill. I really do quite like the little female kitten though. She so reminds me of myself, don't you think?'

Felix shook his head in disbelief and the chain on the collar rattled.

At that moment, the guard, whom Sophia had sent for food, arrived back with a tray in hand. He stopped when he came across the two of them sitting on the floor opposite each other. He bowed awkwardly towards Sophia.

'Mistress, the prisoner's food. I brought some salmon and rabbit caught freshly this morning. There is also some spinach and a bowl of milk. There was no cream available.' He showed the tray to Sophia, ignoring Felix completely.

The guard laid the tray down between Sophia and Felix and left the cell. Sophia leaned over and picked a piece of rabbit off the tray.

'Delicious, as always,' she said, licking her pads and cleaning over her whiskers. 'Don't let it go to waste, Felix. Cook will be angry. Here.'

She lifted a piece of salmon and held it out to him. 'Come on, Felix, just like the old days when we used to feed each other. Trust me.'

Felix opened his mouth, baring his fangs, but his eyes never left Sophia's. She fed him the salmon then sat back and licked her own paw.

'So, you were telling me about little Thomas Angel. How is my son? Doing well?'

'I'm not telling you anything about that kitten, other than he is more of a cat now than you will ever be,' said Felix. He was starving but there was no way he was about to touch the food in front of her. On cue, Felix's stomach gave a loud rumble.

'I'll leave you to eat then, seeing as you won't speak to me. The thing is, Felix, I know all about him already.

What he does every day, who his friends are, who he speaks to, who he loves. I. Know. Everything!'

'You didn't even know the colour of his fur! You thought you knew everything before, Sophia, remember?' replied Felix, 'and you were wrong on that occasion too. Leave Tom to get on with his life. He doesn't know anything about the Ce, or you, and I doubt he even cares. He has friends and a life in Edinburgh. Leave him be.'

'You think he'll want to leave it be when he knows the power he could have? Do you, Felix? Have you not learnt the lessons of the past either? What cat would give up being the master of all the Cait of Ce, just so he can live a quiet life with little Miss Pretty and his little friends? Shall I tell you? Not a single cat I know. Not you, not I, not Flynn or your precious Claudia. We are all greedy, we all want what we can't have.'

'Are you talking about the Ce still, or something else entirely?' said Felix, shaking his head. 'You're wrong, Sophia. I would have given up everything for you. I would have given up my life. I had already given it up for you. There was never anyone else, but you would never listen to me about Claudia. It was your own doing – you created this maelstrom of hate and death and destruction. Look where we are, what we are doing to each other. Kasperi would never have wanted this. This is all of your own doing.'

Felix was knocked sideways by a slap to his face.

His face grazed the floor, and as he tried to get up, Sophia put her knee on his chain, keeping him where he was. She leaned close into him.

'Never mention my father's name again, you understand me? You are not worthy of saying his name.'

Once again, they were whisker to whisker like sweethearts, then Sophia spat in Felix's face before flouncing out of the cell, banging the door shut behind her.

The door of the bathroom opened, and Meissa walked in and sat down on the stool beside the bath.

'So,' she said, as Tom tried his best to retain his modesty. She glanced over at him trying to cover his whole body with two wet paws and a scrawny wet tail and sighed.

Tom remained stock-still in the bath.

'What do we do now?' she said, staring into the middle distance.

'What do you mean, what do we do now?' he said, trying to edge his way over to a towel. Meissa ignored him and carried on talking, oblivious to him.

'If Felix is dead, then what happens to the Order? I mean, I suppose it carries on - it has done for hundreds of years - but who does it get handed on to? He doesn't have any family, does he? Goodness, I know so little about him, and Claudia is in no state to tell me anything at all.'

'How is she?' he asked, claw tips inches from the towel.

'I've never seen anyone so devastated. She's in pieces. What can we do? To help her, I mean. What do you know about Claudia, Tom? I know I spent some time with her when I was seeing Zachariah, but it's not as though we had in-depth chats about her past or her family or really anything important. It was all just chit-chat really.'

She leant over and handed Tom the towel without even looking at him.

'Thanks.'

'I just don't know what to do now. The vet has given her a sedative and that will make her sleep for a few hours, but what happens then? Where do we go from here?'

'What are you two talking about?' said Zachariah's voice from the doorway of the bathroom.

'Do you mind?' Tom said, trying to cover himself in the bath with the towel. 'I can't talk about this now, with you two in here with me!'

'You're right, friend. And we wouldn't want anything going wrinkly in the bathwater now, would we? Not in front of Meissa.' Zachariah smirked, suppressing a laugh.

Tom blushed to the tip of his tail, but Meissa just sat there in her own little world.

'Meissa,' said Zachariah, 'I think Tom would like to get out of the bath now.' He turned to leave the room.

'Oh! Gosh! Oh! Sorry! I didn't realise!' she stammered, blushing as deeply as Tom had done, and she rushed out the room with her head in her paws.

A few minutes later, dried and well and truly wrapped in a robe, Tom came back into the sitting room where Zachariah was once again dozing by the fire. He could still feel the burning in his cheeks as Meissa tapped the arm of the chair she was sitting in. He went over and sat on the floor in front of her seat, his back being warmed by the fire. She was deep in thought.

'What do you think the Ce's next move will be?' she asked, moving back in the seat, pulling her legs up and wrapping her tail round them. Tom noticed she had quite a short tail for her height. 'If there is no Felix to stop them, and the Order haven't got a hierarchy in place, then the Ce will be able to take over completely, without so much as a fight.'

He gazed up at her and nodded, only half-listening. He was daydreaming he was kissing her and running his paws through her fur.

'What do you think of Sophia?' she asked, then paused, waiting for an answer.

'What?' Tom said, suddenly realising she was talking to him.

'Sophia? Is she mad, or just a cat looking for revenge?'

'Mad – totally and utterly deranged,' Tom said, nodding his head to show that whatever she was saying he was in total agreement with.

'I don't think she is,' Meissa said. 'All that time I spent with her at the broch, she kept me close to her and, yes, she's a bit unhinged, but if she were as insane as you all seem to think, then she wouldn't be in charge of a fighting force the way she is. And believe me, Tom, she is the one in charge, absolutely. Those cats do her bidding, whatever she asks of them. If she so much as showed a chink in her armour they would be all over her, but they're not. They are scared of her, but at the same time she is such a great military leader that they trust her. It's her birthright.'

'She's very beautiful,' Tom said, the words out of his mouth before he realised what he had said. 'I keep having the feeling I've seen her before somewhere, but I'm not sure where.'

'What's that got to do with it?'

'I don't know. I suppose I just expect leaders of warrior cats to be big tomcats with battle scars, not beautiful, elegant, slim queens, with stunning eyes.'

'Oh, so she's got stunning eyes, does she?' Meissa laughed. 'That's a very sexist attitude, you know, Tom Angel. There will be none of that talk here, thank you,' she chided, but she was still laughing.

They decided the best option was to speak to Ash.

After all, who knew Felix better than his own butler? He must surely know what the set-up was with the Order, and who was next in line to lead. Then they would work out a plan of action to bring Felix back, whether he was dead or alive. Tom woke Zachariah, who snorted in fright, then he toddled off to have a bath, which was just as well as he was now starting to smell like a mixture of damp woods, sea salt, and fish, altogether not a pleasant combination.

By now, Tom had a ravenous appetite. Meissa accompanied him downstairs and into the dining room to see what pickings were left from earlier. Unfortunately for them, Agatha had already cleared up, so they ended up raiding the kitchen to find some leftovers and made a very handsome meal for themselves of cold ham, cheese and boiled eggs.

Agatha came in to find them in the middle of their little feast all spread out on the kitchen table.

'Mistress Claudia won't be happy,' she said. 'She doesn't approve of snacking between meals.'

Tom exchanged a glance with Meissa who had the beginnings of a smile on her whiskers.

'I'm sure this once, Claudia will let it slide, Agatha,' he said, finishing off the last of the ham as Zachariah came into the kitchen.

'This is where the pair of you got to!' Zachariah

said. 'I was beginning to wonder if you had sneaked off without me.' He took a bite of cheese and Agatha smacked his paw. He was too quick for her and grabbed her paw between his and kissed it.

'Dear Agatha, thank you from the bottom of my heart. You really are a most wonderful cook.'

Agatha blushed as Zachariah winked at her and then kissed her paw again before letting go of it.

'But now we must take our leave,' he said, and tugged his imaginary forelock before ushering them all out of the room, leaving Agatha speechless in his wake.

The three of them grabbed coats and hurried out into the early evening. The wind whipped Tom's face, bringing back the memory of the boat trip from Cataibh. He reached out and took Meissa's paw and secretly vowed to himself that no matter what, he would bring Felix back home to the people he loved, and who loved him. Meissa squeezed his paw back and peeked at him from under the hood of her cape. Tom felt his heart soar and knew that no matter what lay ahead or where he had to go, Meissa would always be by his side.

The three of them walked the short distance to Felix's house with speed, but when they reached the now familiar door and Zachariah banged the knocker, no one answered. The house seemed empty of life, even the street was silent as they waited. They tried again to no avail. Eventually, just as Zachariah was about to try to open the door himself and enter, the door swung open, but it wasn't Ash who was standing there with open arms as usual, waiting to take their coats and welcome them in.

Felix stood in the open doorway. That is, it looked like Felix, but it wasn't him. This cat had the same height, the same rich chocolate coat, but the eyes weren't the same bright blue and the build was slimmer. The voice, when he spoke though, sounded like Felix speaking.

'Ah, good evening. I'm guessing you three must be Tom, Zachariah and Meissa. Ash has told me all about you. Please come in.'

The cat stood back from the door, and they walked into the hallway as usual, taking off their coats but rather awkwardly holding them, with no Ash to give them to.

'You must forgive me,' said the chocolate cat, holding his arms out for their coats. 'Ash has just popped out for a few minutes on a little errand for me, and I am forgetting my manners. Felix would be most upset if I didn't welcome his friends in his usual manner.'

He walked over to a door, and opening it, found the library. He tried another, but this time it led to the dining room.

'Think you might try that one,' said Tom, pointing to a door tucked into the recess of the staircase.

The cat walked over and, finding a closet, quickly hung the coats up. They stood in silence, watching him.

'I suppose you're wondering who I am, the lost soul in the Order's HQ,' he said, his back to them. 'I do apologise, but it's all been a bit hurried. I've just arrived back and found out about Felix. I've landed in the middle of a crisis of sorts, and I've never been good in a crisis, not really.'

He turned to find all three of them standing in the same position as he had left them, agape at him.

'It might be an idea to tell us who you are to begin with,' said Meissa. 'Why don't we go in here until Ash gets back?' She walked over to the library and opened the door, standing back once she had done so.

'Oh no,' said the cat, shaking his head, 'queens first.' He held the door for Meissa who entered, quickly followed by Tom, then Zachariah. Tom's fur bristled as he walked past him. The cat shut the door and sat down in an empty seat. They sat in an awkward silence until Meissa spoke again.

'I'm terribly sorry, but you still haven't told us who you are,' she said, reaching out and touching his paw.

'Oh, my apologies. I'm Edward De'Ath. I'm Felix's brother. I've been over in the Far East, you know, after the War, keeping an eye on the Cait of Ce. I received a few messages from Felix, telling me they were getting more violent over here. Well, I didn't know what to do, so

I jumped on the first steamer back, with the intention of helping Felix with what I could. I'm kind of out of the loop with what's happening with the Order over here. It's been a number of years since I've been back in the country, and well, you know, things happen.'

'They certainly do, Edward, they certainly do,' said Zachariah, chuckling to himself.

Tom had found himself staring at Edward as he spoke. His mannerisms were similar to Felix's, but where Felix was strong and knowledgeable, Edward seemed hesitant with every word he spoke. Cats would follow Felix to the end of the earth, but Tom wasn't sure if they would follow Edward to the end of the street.

'Are you Felix's younger brother?' he asked, dropping into the conversation.

Edward looked over at him.

'Why, yes I am. Felix is two years older than I. You must be Tom,' he said, as though seeing him for the first time.

Tom nodded.

'Hmm.'

'Hmm? What's that mean? Has Felix spoken about me?' Tom asked.

'Oh yes, he's mentioned all of you. He's quite proud of your achievements, Tom. Says you have a natural talent. Doesn't understand why they are trying to hunt you down and kill you though. That is a bit of a mystery. I've heard nothing, over in China, I mean. It's very perplexing.'

The front door banged open and shut. Tom, Meissa and Zachariah all shot out of their seats and into the hallway to be greeted by Ash.

'Good evening, gentlecats,' he said. 'I see Edward has introduced himself. May I get you some cream or a little milk?'

'That would be lovely, Ash,' replied Meissa, 'and whilst you're at it, make one for yourself. I think we have some talking to do.'

They returned to the library and made idle chit-chat with Edward until Ash came in bearing a tray laden with cream and snacks.

'Edward was just telling us all about China and the Catnip Wars, Ash,' said Meissa, as he poured out the glasses of thick gloopy cream.

Ash's hand paused for a second then carried on pouring the cream.

'That was a long time ago, Miss,' he said, returning the jug to the tray.

'Well, I think you and Edward need to sit down and tell us all about it, don't you? Because whatever happened there is having an impact on what is happening here, right now.'

'There is nothing to tell,' said Ash, his face changing from friendly to professional in the blink of an eye.

'As I said, the Cait of Ce have been prevalent over there for years,' interrupted Edward. 'There was a dispute between local warlords in China over catnip crops and we got caught in the middle of it. It ended up being very messy, but thankfully we all came back alive.'

'What happened between Felix and Sophia?' Meissa asked.

'Not much, as I understand it. They had been young cats in love, but it was all over before we ended up there I think. She was said to have had a dalliance with one of her warriors or someone, but nothing much came of it, and she disappeared for a bit only to turn up a while later in Scotland. That's about it. We fought, some died, and still it goes on, a never-ending cycle of hate and greed. Felix would turn his back on it in a heartbeat, but the Ce won't let us. We spend all our time trying to stop them destroying communities and countries and spreading their evil ways.' Edward stretched out his paws and yawned. 'Sorry, it's been a long day.'

'What about my Aunt Claudia? What did she do? Did she fight them too?' asked Zachariah, ignoring Edward's hint for them to leave.

'Ah, the beautiful Claudia,' said Edward, smiling to himself. 'I think we were all a bit in love with her. She was strong and intelligent and all the things that make young cats fall head over heels in love with queens, but she was never interested in us. Had eyes for one cat only – but Felix only saw her as a friend. That's the way of the world, I suppose. Once the war had ended, Felix and Claudia headed towards Tibet before going their separate ways. Made her fortune in diamonds, although I do believe there were other stories around at the time, that she did mercenary work, and worked for whoever gave the biggest pay cheque, but as I say, it may have only been rumour.' He yawned again, and this time Ash also made a move.

They all stood up to leave, but Meissa stopped before she got to the door.

'What about Felix, how do we get him back?' she said to Edward. 'You must know the Ce and how they operate. What will Sophia do with him?'

Edward laughed, but it was an ironic, hollow laugh.

'If Sophia hasn't changed, and by all accounts she's been getting worse, not better, then there is no point in worrying about Felix. She'll have killed him already, and knowing Sophia, she will have enjoyed every minute of it.'

The whole way back to Claudia's, Meissa was inconsolable. Tom tried to comfort her by telling her that Edward was wrong, that Felix was alive and not to worry about what he had said. But he knew from the glances exchanged between himself and Zachariah that they were both thinking the same thing; that if Felix's own brother thought he was dead, then he probably was. What did they know, two silly little kittens out of the orphanage, playing at being warriors? Tom thought about what had happened since he had come to stay with Claudia. She was now a broken cat, and Lord alone knew if she would ever recover. Meissa's parents had been tortured and killed, she had been kidnapped and held hostage by Sophia, and now Felix had been captured, and possibly killed. All because the Cait of Ce wanted him. What did they want with him? Why was he so valuable to them? Tom had no idea – it seemed no one had. All he knew was that everything had happened because of him.

SIXTEEN

Flynn came into Felix's cell and woke him.

'Felix, are you awake? Come on, I'm to take you to Sophia.'

Felix yawned, stretched and let out a yowl of pain when his muscles protested at the movement. Rubbing his whiskers, he looked up at his old friend.

'What now, Flynn. What is she up to this time? Can she just not leave it be?' He moved to get up as Flynn unlocked the collar. Felix rubbed at the sores on his neck. He was starting to go bald in places with the friction. 'I'm beginning to hope she'll kill me, just to finish it once and for all.'

'You don't mean that!' said Flynn, putting down a tray of trout in front of Felix. 'Eat this. You'll need your strength. She's summoned a few of her best men, but I don't know what she's planning on. She's told no one. That is, if you don't count talking to her dead father every night.' Flynn leant against the wall and watched as Felix hurriedly ate the food.

'Is she still having the nightmares?' Felix asked, taking another piece of trout and washing it down with water.

Flynn nodded. 'I'm surprised you don't get woken with her screaming. It wakes the rest of the broch. Her demons stalk her night and day, Felix. It's not good.' Flynn looked down at his paws. 'I worry about her.'

Felix stopped with a piece of fish halfway to his mouth. 'You should tell her, Flynn. She thinks she's alone in the world and that no one loves her.'

'You think there's a reason for her thinking that?' said Flynn, a twinkle in his eye. Felix laughed, but he had been serious.

'Did you know Tom was her kitten?'

'It crossed my mind, but I didn't know for sure. Kasperi came to me one night and asked me to take a kitten to an orphanage, which I did, but I didn't know he was Sophia's. He does look like her though.'

'Who's Tom's father?'

Flynn shrugged. 'You knew Kasperi. You didn't ask questions. You just did as you were told or suffer the consequences. I never asked, and I wasn't told.'

'Why didn't you tell me, Flynn? That he was Sophia's? I could have protected him from all this.'

'You've got to understand, Felix, I didn't even know who this Thomas Angel was until I saw him that day in Claudia's house. We were just told to find a kitten called Thomas Angel, living in Edinburgh. I didn't even put two and two together until I'd seen him. He has those beautiful eyes of hers, but even then, it could have been just my imagination. I didn't want to say something in case I was wrong.'

'You should have told me.'

Flynn sighed. 'You nearly finished?' He indicated the nearly empty tray. 'We'll need to be going, and we both know she doesn't like to be kept waiting now, does she?'

Felix scooped up the rest of the trout into his mouth and slowly started to stand up. He had been chained to the floor for days now, and pain seared through his body as he tried to lengthen his limbs. Once he had eased himself into a standing position, he nodded to Flynn.

'Okay, let's go.'

Sophia was pacing up and down in the meeting hall, while a dozen of her warriors were warming themselves by the hearth. She looked over as Felix and Flynn entered the hall. Flynn handed Felix a cloak.

'Think you'll be needing this,' he said, eyeing up Sophia. She was wearing a full-length cloak with breeches and boots underneath. 'Looks like we're going on a trip.'

'About time!' shouted Sophia at Flynn. 'I don't appreciate being made to wait around for a prisoner.'

'My apologies, mistress,' said Flynn, bowing low in front of her. Felix, knowing what Sophia was like when she was in one of these moods, followed suit.

'Greer, is it ready?'

'Yes, mistress,' Greer said, trying to make himself as small as possible so Sophia wouldn't notice him too much.

She brushed past him without so much as a backward glance and strode up the stairs to the rooftop. Flynn, Felix and the Ce warriors followed. The sun was setting on the horizon, the sky turning from blue to a pink blush. Felix breathed in the fresh, cold air. He looked around, wondering what they were waiting for. At that moment, from behind a mountain that cradled the broch, rose an airship, the copper-coloured skin glinting in the setting sun. It glided over to the broch and gently settled onto the roof, the only sound a soft whirr, like a cat purring. The door to the gondola opened and Sophia strode inside.

'Wow, I had no idea!' said Felix, as he walked inside with Flynn and sat down in the fur-lined seats in the cabin.

'Get moving, I haven't got all day!' shouted Sophia at the stragglers. With the warriors inside, the door closed with a click, and the airship lifted from the roof and began its journey.

Once they were up in the air, Sophia summoned Flynn over to where she was sitting, a little apart from the rest of the group. Felix watched them as they whispered together, their ears almost touching. Flynn suddenly stood up, shaking his head, and walked back to where Felix was seated.

'All she'll say is that we are going to Edinburgh.' He glanced up at Felix. 'Other than that, she won't discuss her plans. She says we either fight with her or against her. Our choice.'

Felix heard no murmurings of dissent from the other warriors, but then he realised that Sophia, although she looked to all intents and purposes like she was snuggling into her seat, was actually watching the faces of the cats to see their reactions. Sophia caught Felix watching her and gave him a little smile, but it chilled him to the bone. He knew that if Sophia was heading towards Edinburgh, it could only mean trouble for Tom and the rest of the Order, and with Flynn with him, there was no way of letting them know that Sophia was on her way. His one hope was that Sophia had let her plan slip to someone in the broch who was an ally of the Order, otherwise there would be no way to warn them to prepare themselves. And if they didn't find out, it would be a bloodbath.

Felix watched as Sophia snuggled into the chair and closed her eyes. How could she want to kill Tom, her own kitten, he wondered, as he looked at her beautiful face, so peaceful in rest? Flynn glanced over at Felix then followed his gaze to watch Sophia.

As the sky steadily grew dark outside, the airship purred on. Tipping the edge of Loch Ness, the airship banked slightly and turned towards the Cairngorm mountains, rising higher so as not to clip the top of Ben Macdui. The stars carpeted the black sky, but Felix couldn't think of anything other than those innocent cats he loved, sitting at home in Edinburgh, unaware of who or what was about to descend on them. The darkness was so intense that Felix had no idea where they were until the airship began to descend and he looked out to see that they were over the Forth Rail Bridge, its bright red spires shooting heavenward, the waters of the Forth below it, black and icy. As they continued on their journey, the fields and open spaces gave way to townhouses and roads, and as the airship got lower and lower, Felix could see the familiar cobblestones on the streets of the New Town.

Sophia stretched and let out a long meow. As the airship hovered, then slowly lowered to the ground in the gardens of Moray Place, the cats readied themselves. With a gentle bump the ship landed, and the door opened out for them to exit. Sophia led the way. She stalked through the gardens silently. Felix could feel his pulse racing and he slowed his breathing to calm himself. He could feel the electricity in the air – these cats were pumped for a fight. They followed Sophia through the gate of the gardens and came face-to-face with a familiar front door. It was Claudia's.

Seventeen

They stood shoulder to shoulder staring at the darkened house on the other side of the street.

'Sophia,' said Felix, walking over to her and putting his paw on her shoulder, 'what are you doing? Think about this. What will you gain by killing Tom?'

She turned to look at him, then down at his paw on her. Felix removed his paw but stayed standing where he was. She looked back up at his face. Her eyes were empty, like she was there in body, but her mind was elsewhere.

'What will I gain?' she said. 'My life.'

'What? You'll get your life back by taking his? That's madness, Sophia, even you know that!'

'Do I, Felix? All I know is right now, and ever since I found out he was alive, I've done nothing but think about it. The kittens I drowned have haunted me every night and every day since Kasperi told me he lived. I see their faces, Felix, hear their mewling as I did it, and I know that unless I get rid of him they will continue to haunt me. As long as he lives, I can't move on. Can't you see? There is no other way.'

Felix pulled her round to face him.

'And what happens if Tom Angel haunts you every night after that? You'll get no peace by killing him, Sophia. Don't do this to yourself. You can have other kittens if you want – you're still young enough – just don't kill Tom.'

'You're so sweet, Felix, but you won't change my mind. You can't protect your little kitten, Felix.'

She shrugged herself out of his grip and threw off her cloak. The other cats who had been watching their exchange, prickled with the anticipation of a fight, albeit one against a sleeping queen, three kittens and a serving cat.

Sophia took a flying leap, landing on the first floor balconette, whilst the others leapt and took positions at other windows. On her nod, they all opened the locked windows using their senses. Then one by one they disappeared inside except Felix who was left standing on the pavement outside. It was inky black and silent for a few seconds then the whole house seemed to explode into light and noise. Everywhere Felix looked he could see movement and flashes. Running to the front door, he tried to kick it open, but it swung open just as his boot touched it. He half-sprang, half-fell into the hallway to be greeted by Flynn who was on the other side of the door.

'I thought Claudia would be seriously peeved if you kicked down her door,' he said by way of explanation.

Closing the door quietly, Flynn and Felix then ran up the stairs where most of the noise was coming from, only to be greeted by a ruffled Tarquair fighting tooth and claw with one of the Ce warriors. As they rolled past Felix as one single hissing bundle of fur, he saw Tarquair lift his head, open his mouth and sink his teeth into the other cat's scruff in a very unfriendly manner. The pair of them hit the bannister with a sickening thud then began a slow roll down the stairs, still knotted together.

A loud painful yowl echoed around the central hall and Flynn ran in the direction of the noise. Felix paused for a moment, undecided whether he should try and find Claudia, Sophia or Tom first. Then he ran for the stairs that took him to the second floor and Tom and Zachariah's rooms.

Up on the second floor all was quiet. The lights were out and it was dark as pitch. Felix could barely see his paw in front of his whiskers, so he focused on using his senses to acclimatise himself to his surroundings. He walked slowly from room to room, entering silently and then scanning the room to see if he could see or even sense anyone else there. The sitting room was empty, even the fire was dead. The chairs sat where they normally would, everything was as it should be – it was all too normal. Felix walked to the bathroom and pushed the door open; nothing. Tom's bedroom was next and as he entered he could sense someone was in the room with him. Felix could make out a figure lying at an awkward angle on the bed, half on the bed, half on the floor.

'No!' he yelled, running to its side. 'Tom!' He put his arms around the body, and holding it close to him, he felt his fur become wet and sticky. 'No!'

He turned the body over with some difficulty. Lifeless eyes looked back at him, and the fur was beginning to lose its gloss. The life force that shines from every living being was dulled as the life slowly ebbed from the cat. Felix stifled a sob as it rose involuntarily from his throat. The tears started to roll down his cheeks as he slowly put the cat back on the bed.

'Thank goodness,' he said, recognising the cat.

It wasn't Tom but one of the Ce cats who had travelled with them.

'How touching,' said a voice from behind him.

He turned to see Sophia in shadow blocking the doorway.

'You heartless bitch! That's one of your own and

you couldn't care less!' Felix wiped the tears with his paw and dragged himself to standing.

Sophia uttered a mirthless laugh. Raging with anger, Felix sprang on her. He bit Sophia's scruff, forcing her head back and her paws outstretched. Momentarily she was stunned, then she twisted her body, so it was she on top of Felix, biting his face and neck. Felix flailed with his paw to stop her and smacked her on her nose, causing her to stumble backwards and lose her grip on him. Immediately he was on top of her, pinning her to the floor and trying to bite her neck, but she kept squirming out of his grasp. Wriggling away, Sophia backed off for a moment, panting but watching him all the time.

'So, you like it rough do you, Felix?' she said. 'Good.'

She launched herself back onto him landing on his back and biting him on the scruff. Felix twisted and turned his neck, the weal's from his jail collar breaking open to bleed as he did so. Unable to get a grip on her, Felix stopped moving, his breath ragged. As he lay there, he felt Sophia's grip ease ever so slightly and as soon as it had, he used the opportunity to twist from her grip and turn so he was biting her in the stomach. He could feel his teeth break the skin and taste her blood as it started to ooze into his mouth. He couldn't kill her, not like this. He had loved this cat once – in a way he still loved her – but right now it was going to be him or her. She was going for the kill no matter what Felix did. He lessened his bite on her and she bolted away in pain, then turned and flung herself at him once more. They were both exhausted, but Sophia caught Felix on his lower back and, sinking her teeth in, held him there. The pain scorched through his body and he felt all his strength leaving him. His head drooped as he feigned submission, and the split second her teeth lifted slightly, Felix slid out from underneath to face her. They both were breathing out low guttural growls, ears flattened against their heads as they circled each other, keeping each other in view at all times. Felix had never imagined fighting Sophia like this. They had had their fights like all couples but never a down-and-dirty, rolling-about-on-the-ground physical fight before. He looked at her – her eyes were full of hatred, the pupils wild and dilated. Her mouth was pulled back, showing her teeth and fangs, her nose wrinkled. This wasn't the Sophia he knew; this was some mad cat on the edge of insanity, and he knew in that instant that she would kill him and think nothing of it. The second his mind slipped from the fight, Sophia pounced. She leapt over him, taking him by surprise, but then twisted mid-air and landed on his back with her full weight bringing him crashing to the ground, her fangs sinking deep into his throat. He felt them push harder, bursting the skin and crushing his windpipe. He tried to move but couldn't – he couldn't breathe, and the room started to swirl around him. Felix could feel the life start to leave his body. With every shallow breath he took, Sophia bit down harder, killing Felix slowly but surely. The darkness of the room became heightened to him and he started to see a myriad of colours everywhere, but he knew he was seeing things, that this was the last thing he would ever see. He thought of little Tom and felt saddened that he wouldn't be able to save him after all. Then everything went black.

'No!' The scream punctuated the black.

Felix felt his head bounce. Again, another yell – it seemed to come from very far away but at the same time seemed very loud to him. He felt the weight lift from him and heard a horrendous thud as something landed against the far wall by the bed. The next thing he was aware of, was Tom, right beside him, his paws around him. He felt warmth surge through his body. Felix tried to think why his fur would feel sticky, but his head was too fuzzy to come up with an answer.

EIGHTEEN

Tom ran into the room to find Sophia straddling Felix and biting down on his neck, crushing his windpipe. He yelled out, distracting her into letting her grip loosen for a second, but a second was long enough for him to grab her and propel her across the room. Sophia was stunned but shook herself, and although unsteady on her paws, managed to pull herself upright. He went over to Felix to see if he was still alive.

'My, my,' she said, 'isn't this a touching little family reunion?'

Tom looked up from Felix, puzzled.

'Mummy and Daddy and their little baby kitten. How sweet.'

'What?' he said, thinking he had heard her wrongly.

'That's no way to greet your mother after all these years, Thomas,' Sophia said, smiling at the fact she had shocked him to the core.

'The locket!'

That's where he had seen Sophia before. It was her picture that was in Tom's locket.

'Felix is my father?' Tom said, still looking at Felix, but his question was to Sophia.

'Never mind Felix!' she shouted, throwing a nearby brush at him. 'This is about me! Not him!'

Tom could feel tears well in his eyes, but at the same time he couldn't stop smiling. Felix was smiling back at him, still breathless, but now grinning from ear-to-ear.

'I said, ignore him!' Sophia screamed at Tom. She raised her paw and as she did so Felix flew from Tom's grasp and across the room where he hit the wall and slid to the floor.

'Don't you dare touch my father!' Tom yelled, but at the same time as feeling his anger for Sophia, he felt this whoop of pure joy when he said the word, "father". He raised his paw towards Sophia and a burst of energy surged from him, hitting her square in the chest, and she was flung back over the bed. Almost immediately she was back on her paws and coming for him. Tom paused for a moment, aware that Felix was still in the room with her, then made a run for it. He had barely got a few steps when her weight on his back brought him crashing down to the floor face first. She sank her fangs into him, then suddenly let go and started hitting him all over with her paws, her claws out, slashing him all over. Lying face down there was nothing he could do but take the battering that she was giving him. He tried to cover his head as best as he could, but he felt a powerful slash cut through his ear and he yowled out in pain. All the while she was doing this, Sophia was screaming at him. It was hard for Tom to make out the words, but she seemed to be blaming him for everything and anything.

Suddenly, she stopped screaming and hitting him. She stood up but stayed standing over him. Tom looked up at her, waiting for the next slap, which didn't come. Instead, she spat on him.

'I should have made sure you drowned,' she said, before swinging her leg back and landing a perfect winding kick right into his stomach.

Tom lay motionless, waves of pain shooting through his body. What had he done to deserve this? What did she mean, "I should have made sure you drowned?" How could this cat be his mother? His mother was dead, and even if she wasn't, why would she hate him so much? It just didn't make sense. He rolled over and was sick on the carpet.

Agatha would have his guts for garters, he thought.

He became aware of a movement above him and he glanced up just in time to see something – he wasn't sure what it was – come straight for his head. He moved at the last minute, managing to miss both the object and the pile of vomit. He struggled to get to his paws, but as soon as he tried to stand, Sophia kicked them away from him again.

'Come on, Thomas, let me have some fun before I kill you. You're making it too easy for me. I'll kill you first and then Felix.' She swung her leg back to take another kick, but Tom caught it before it hit him and twisted it back on itself, causing her to yowl in pain this time. She fell to the floor and he was on her back in an instant. He felt a hatred like he had never felt before surge through him. She may or may not be his mother, but he was sure as hell she wasn't going to take his father away from him all over again. With his claws embedded in her neck, he leaned in closely to her.

'You forget, Sophia, I am my mother's son.' And he stuck his claws in deeper, feeling her flinch in pain. He felt her relax under his grip for a moment, then she managed to wriggle free and was sinking her teeth into his scruff before he realised what was happening. He flailed for a moment, his mind whirling through scenarios of how he could get her off his back, and then he realised what he needed to do. He tried to focus his mind, just as Felix had taught him, and let the energy come through his body. He could feel the white heat pulsing through his bones, leeching its way into his limbs and paws, and he could feel the power that he had within him. Sophia's grip on his scruff had lessened as he concentrated on his energy until she completely let go of him and started to back away from him.

'What the hell?' she said, in complete shock at what she was seeing.

Tom could see himself shining. He seemed to glow from head to foot, his ginger fur now golden and shimmering. He looked over at Sophia standing, mouth open, disbelieving what she was seeing. Behind her, he could see Felix come out of the room, still holding his throat. His face was a mixture of shock, wonder and happiness. Tom stood looking at the pair of them, his parents, and nearly laughed and lost his focus for a moment. How ridiculous this whole situation was. He felt like he was the one with the upper hand, the one with the power. Sophia, coming to her senses and realising Felix was behind her, spun round and grabbed him, putting her claw to his throat.

'Thomas, whatever you're doing, stop it,' she said, pressing the claw in deeper, so it drew blood. 'Stop it now, or I kill Felix, and I mean it this time.'

Tom had to laugh at her – he had no idea what he

was doing, or even how to control it. At the mention of her killing Felix, he felt a rush of pain and for a second he glowed brighter. Sophia gasped, then continued her stance.

'I mean it, Thomas. You know I won't give killing him a second thought.'

Tom glanced at Felix, who despite being held by Sophia was still staring at him in amazement, a half-smile still on his lips.

'Don't listen to her, Tom. Remember what I taught you. No matter what happens, don't let the Ce win.'

Sophia drew her claw across Felix's throat. He dropped to the floor and remained there, not moving.

'No!' Tom cried, looking down at Felix lying motionless on the floor between them. Sophia started to laugh, and prodded Felix's body with the toe of her boot.

'You killed him! You murderous bitch! You're not worthy of being my mother. It should have been you who was drowned, not me! And Felix is worth a million of you!' he yelled at her, realising his childish rant had no effect on her. What did have an effect on her was what was happening to his body. The more Tom screamed and shouted at her, the brighter he shone, until he could see himself glow like an angel, white and gold, with pure brilliance. Sophia stopped laughing at him and stared open-mouthed. Then she started mumbling to herself, talking as though someone were whispering in her ear. This in itself baffled Tom. Who the hell was she talking to? She started to try and back away from him, all the while mumbling to herself.

'Get back here!' he shouted, and all of a sudden she seemed to be pulled back in front of him. At this she became hysterical. Sophia desperately tried to get away, screaming and twisting and shouting, but all the while it was like she was held in place invisibly. Tom watched her as she became more and more frantic, trying to fight the invisible hand holding her just where he wanted her. She was a cat possessed. Tom stared in disbelief as she flailed and kicked out at unseen hands holding her. In the midst of her flailing, her foot kicked Felix and he rolled onto his back, his eyes staring up. Tom looked down at him and thought that he no longer wanted to know of her existence – and to his utter amazement, no sooner did he have that thought than Sophia was sent flying across the room, missing the window by inches, but flying into the window frame and knocking her unconscious.

As he stood there, with two unconscious and possibly dead cats at his paws – Tom's new-found parents, he was at a loss as to what to do. He went to Felix first and lifted him into his arms.

'Felix, can you hear me?' Tom tenderly whispered in his ear. There was no response. 'Please, Felix, don't die.

Please don't leave me just when I've found you.'

Tom put his face into the scruff of Felix's neck and breathed in his scent. He started to cry, the tears melting into Felix's fur.

'You'll make me soggy if you keep doing that,' said a croaky voice.

'Felix! Oh, you're alive!' Tom whooped with joy and hugged him even tighter.

'Don't do that,' Felix croaked huskily, 'I think I've broken a rib or two.' He started to smile and chuckle, then winced in pain and held his side. 'Don't make me laugh,' he said, wincing again.

'Okay, Dad,' Tom said, grinning from ear-to-ear.

'Okay, son,' Felix replied, returning his smile.

A floorboard creaked from behind Tom and he turned to see a rather dishevelled Claudia standing behind them in the doorway.

'Should I ask why you two are lying wrapped in each other's arms on the floor? Actually, I don't want to know. I just want to hug both of you. I thought you were dead, Felix,' she said, her voice shaking with emotion. She paused to compose herself. 'I knew in my heart you weren't. Come here.' She stretched out her paws to him, and Felix, battered and bruised, went to her and they hugged for a long time.

'Come here, Tom,' she said, indicating to him with

a free paw to come over to her.

Tom went to them and they both brought him in to their bear hug. He could have burst with joy; he felt so happy in that moment. Two of the people he loved most in the world, one of whom he now knew to be his father, were both here with him. He could feel the energy pulse through his body again and could feel himself start to glow. Felix and Claudia, both with their eyes shut, couldn't see, but someone else in the room could.

'How touching,' said Sophia, voice dripping with sarcasm. 'The little family all back together, how sweet.'

She was standing by the window, but Tom could see she had been hurt. She was holding her arm by her side. Claudia broke free from them and Felix went to grab her paw to hold her back. She shrugged it off and walked over to Sophia.

'You pathetic, conniving deceitful she-devil!' Claudia hissed in her face. 'How dare you try to take our joy away from us. You destroyed my life once before, Sophia – was that not enough for you? Do you really want to try and do it all again? Because, believe me, just give me one reason, just one little princessy paw out of place, and I will drag you down into the pit of hell and leave you there. Don't think I won't!'

'My, my, haven't we got all bad tempered in old age? Felix always made me happy and relaxed. Doesn't seem he can do the same for you now, does it?' replied Sophia.

Tom didn't see the kick coming, but no sooner were the words out of Sophia's mouth, than Claudia was on top of her, kicking her repeatedly in the head with her back legs. She was like a cat possessed. Tom had never seen her so much as lose her temper with himself or Zachariah, but the fury that she showed towards Sophia was unbelievable! This was about far more than name-calling between queens – this was a fight to the death. They rolled from window to bedside to chest of drawers and back again. Tom stood aghast; he went to separate them, but Felix put his paw on Tom's shoulder.

'Leave them be,' he said. 'They need to get this out of their systems.'

As they rolled and bit and scratched and fought, they hissed and yowled like Tom had never heard cats before. The noise coming from them was primal, evil in an instinctual way. This was no high-bred cats having a paw fight, this was mortal combat. Claudia took a swipe at Sophia with her claws extended and caught her a blow to her chest. An arc of blood sprayed the room and Sophia mewled like it was her last. Tom gasped, broke free from Felix's grip, and ran over to them. This cat may have wanted him dead, but she was still his mother. Startled by the sudden movement behind her, Claudia looked round and seizing the opportunity, Sophia made a bolt for the window, only to be caught by her tail by Claudia.

'I'm not finished with you yet, bitch!' she screamed at her, dragging Sophia back down to the floor.

Tom stopped where he was, mesmerised by them both. They were out for the kill and although they were both exhausted, neither of them was willing to admit defeat. Claudia had lost all awareness of sense as every ounce of hatred for Sophia was channelled into the struggle.

Claudia was using her senses to outwit Sophia at every move. Each time Sophia went to move, Claudia was there before her, ready to bite or swipe her. Tom could see Sophia getting more tense, more nervous, which made Claudia all the bolder. All the while the pair of them yowled and growled at each other, baring their teeth and arching their backs as a warning sign. They circled each other in the room before flying in unison at each other, colliding mid-air and falling to the ground as one. Once more they were a single entity, a mewling hissing ball of fur, moving so fast Tom could hardly keep up with who had the upper paw. First Claudia had Sophia by the throat, then it was Claudia pinned under Sophia, then back to Claudia who was biting Sophia on the stomach. Felix and Tom stood unable to move and barely breathing. Suddenly a voice broke the silence.

'Stop!'

Tom turned to see Edward silhouetted at the door. 'Stop it, both of you!'

Claudia hesitated, distracted for a moment, letting her grip on Sophia slip. Immediately, Sophia wrenched herself from Claudia's claws and threw herself out the window. Tom raced to the window and looked out. Sophia landed with a thump on all four paws on the pavement and regained her balance. Then she tipped her head back and gave out a long, protracted mewl like he had never heard before. From his vantage point, he could see the Ce warriors come running out the house and join her. In a heartbeat they had all leapt the fence and disappeared into the shadow of the gardens.

There was a commotion from outside and Zachariah ran out into the street followed by Meissa and Jones. They were shouting – Zachariah was all for going after them. He kept gesticulating in the direction they had gone and walking over to the fence, trying to see into the gardens. Felix leant past Tom out of the window and whistled down to them. He tried to shout, but his voice wasn't working.

'Tell them to get back inside. They won't catch them now,' he said to Tom with difficulty. 'We need to regroup.'

Tom shouted down to them and although Zachariah was surprised to see him giving orders, he and the others duly came indoors.

As they walked through Claudia's home, Tom saw

for the first time the devastation that a few cats could do. Everywhere there was destruction. Curtains had been ripped down, ornaments smashed, pieces of furniture knocked over or broken. His heart went out to Claudia – all her precious belongings had been destroyed.

She smiled at him, but it was a wan smile. 'They're only possessions, Tom. They don't matter. As long as I have my boys and Felix, everything is fine.' She gave him a little squeeze.

Felix and Edward walked ahead of them and the brothers' likeness was even more apparent than before. Although Edward had his paw round Felix, supporting him as he limped, their mannerisms were strikingly similar. The way they moved their paws when talking, how they put their heads to the side when they laughed, even the way they walked was similar, but not quite identical. Claudia noticed Tom smiling at them.

'You can see they are brothers, can't you?' she whispered in his ear. 'Felix has never got over Edward betraying us though.'

Tom stopped and looked at her. 'Betraying you?'

'Yes, it was Edward who told Sophia that Felix and I were in love all those years ago. If it hadn't been for him, then all our lives would have been so very different.'

'How can Felix still be friendly with him when he destroyed all your lives like that?' Tom asked.

'Because blood will always be thicker than water, Tom, and they are brothers, just as you are Felix's son.'

Tom stopped on the staircase and stared at her.

'How did you know?'

Claudia smiled 'I've thought about it ever since you walked through the door with Zachariah. There was always something so familiar about you, but I couldn't quite put my claw on it. When I saw you both together one day, it was like looking at a younger Felix -except for your colouring, obviously. You must take that from your mother's side. But it was uncanny how alike you were in the way you did things – even your smile. It did lift my heart to see you both so happy in each other's company. But it was too wild an idea. How could you be related to Felix? I knew Edward had never married and Felix had never had kittens, so you couldn't be related to them. I suppose you could have been a cousin or something, but I knew it wasn't that.' She stopped talking and turned to hold Tom's face in both her paws. Her eyes were glistening with tears. 'Felix whispered to me tonight that you were his son. First, I got my beloved Felix back and now he has a son, a wonderful, beautiful, caring son, and I couldn't be happier for both of you.' She kissed Tom gently on both cheeks and a tear rolled down her face.

Tom could feel his face burn with emotion and tears well up in his eyes, but he swallowed them and smiled back at her.

'I'm very happy too, Claudia,' he managed to utter before the tears spilled over and rolled down his cheeks.

'Look at the pair of us!' she said, smiling and wiping away his tears. 'The others will be looking for us. Come on.'

She linked arms with him and they walked down the stairs and into the dining room where the rest of them had gathered.

Shepard was lying on the floor by the windows with bandaging around his stomach. He was awake though and waved across to them as they came into the room. Tarquair and Zachariah were talking to Jones, their heads together, but Tom could still see remnants of hackles up on their fur, and slightly fluffy tails. They were obviously still hyped from the fight. He had just caught a glimpse of Felix and Edward sitting at the dining table talking, when he was grabbed by Meissa, who flung her paws around him and gave him a bear hug, and then kissed him on the lips. Shocked, Tom didn't know what to do; then he kissed her back. She tasted of blood and when they parted he could see why. Her lip was still bleeding from a nasty claw cut. He put his paw up to it and touched it gently.

'Ouch!' she said wincing, but then put her paw on top of his and smiled, before hugging him again.

Tom looked around the room. These were the cats he loved most in the world and he found himself purring unconsciously. They all looked a bit battered and bruised, but he was so glad they were there with him in the room, all alive and well. Meissa snuggled into him. He could feel her purring against his chest, and he felt in that moment like the happiest kitten in the world.

NINETEEN

Felix waved a paw and called everyone to the table. Shepard remained lying on the floor. It seemed his cut was deep, and although it had missed all his vital organs, Meissa wanted to stem the flow of blood before moving him. When they were all seated, Felix began to speak. His voice was still husky, and he sipped from a glass of milk frequently. Tom sat beside Meissa, with Zachariah on his other side, and Jones and Tarquair seated across from him. Claudia was standing beside Felix, her paw on his shoulder; Edward was seated beside him.

'Well, I think we can say with certainty that we aren't safe even here in Edinburgh,' Felix began with a chuckle, 'but seriously, we now know why the Ce are after Tom.' He glanced at him, and Tom nodded. 'He is Sophia's and my kitten.'

Tom could feel the shock in the room, and his tail started to fluff in response to the emotions that he could sense around him. Zachariah slapped him on the back and laughed, and Meissa gave his paw a squeeze. Tarquair placed his paws together and nodded sagely. Jones just looked stunned and Shepard shouted across the room to Felix.

'Felix, you old tom cat, you kept that quiet!'

'Just found out myself, Shepard,' replied Felix, grinning, 'and I couldn't be happier!'

Tom glanced at Edward, and although he too was smiling with the rest of them, Tom sensed something different from what he could see. Tom felt his heart start thumping a little bit faster and he could feel the panic rise in his throat. Edward felt Tom's eyes on him and looked directly at him. In that split second, Tom was chilled to the bone. He shivered. This was his father's brother, his uncle – why was he feeling like this? He swallowed the emotion and dragged himself back into the conversation. Felix, looking like he was about to burst with pride, put his paws up in surrender at the rush of comments he was taking and brought the conversation back to the point in hand.

'Anyway, Sophia is after my son,' he said, and Zachariah whooped and slapped Tom on the back again, 'because he will be next in line to inherit the Cait of Ce when she dies. Tom would be the eleventh generation of ruler, and therefore the most powerful the world has seen. She sees him as a threat and is trying to get him out the way.'

'I don't want anything to do with the Ce,' Tom said, his voice shaking with emotion.

Felix looked at him. 'Tom, you've met your mother – she's not exactly what you would describe as a calm and rational cat. If she thinks something is true, then it's true as far as she's concerned. It doesn't matter how mad the idea is, once she's convinced of it then nothing will shake her from it. As well we know.' Claudia squeezed Felix's shoulder.

Tom glanced back over at Edward, but he was gazing off into the middle distance. How could he betray his brother and their friend to Sophia? What was his motive for doing it? What did he gain? Tom studied Edward's face. It was hard and determined. Tom thought to himself that this cat would do whatever it took to get what he wanted, no matter who was in his way. He took a sharp intake of breath and turned to Meissa who was also looking at Edward with a puzzled look on her face.

'So, we must protect the little ones as much as we can,' Felix was saying. 'They have been through too much already.'

'No offence, Felix, but I think I've proved I can look after myself, once or twice,' Meissa said, only half in jest.

'I know that, little one,' replied Felix. 'We all saw you whip Tom's tail that night, but I think for the time being if we can avoid the fight we will.'

'But Sophia won't avoid a fight just because we're young, Felix. She wants to kill us - me - now when it's easier for her.' Tom butted in, indignant that Felix thought he was too young to fight the Ce after all his training and the battles they had already been through.

'Sophia can kill you any time she chooses.' It was Edward who spoke. He was looking directly at Tom. Tom took Edward's remark as a threat not a statement of fact.

'And I think I've proved that I'm not that easy to kill, Edward. Keep that in mind,' Tom replied, his fur prickling.

'Edward's right,' said Felix. 'She's been thwarted so far, but she'll keep trying until she finds a weakness and then she'll strike again. She got a shock tonight - she wasn't expecting us to be ready for her, but she'll regroup and be back before we know it. Incidentally, how did you know we were going to turn up like that, Tom? Sophia told no one, not even the cats she was with.'

'I don't think we should put anyone's life at risk by telling tales on cats who help us. Didn't you tell me once to trust no one?' Tom said, pointedly looking at Edward.

His ears had pricked up at the talk of traitors.

Felix chuckled. 'Oh, I've taught you too much, little one,' he said, but didn't continue to question how they knew the Ce were coming.

Tom kept his gaze steady on Edward. He was sure as hell he wasn't going to give anyone up to Felix's brother as a sacrificial lamb just to find out if he was a traitor.

Agatha took that moment to enter the room with platters filled with food and the conversation of spies and fighting was forgotten as they all dived into plates full of creamy scrambled eggs and salmon.

Once they were all sated with food, and Shepard's wound had been attended to by a vet, the conversation turned once more to the Cait of Ce.

'What will they do now, Felix?' Tom asked, as he licked the last remnants of salmon from his whiskers.

'Sophia will come back again and again,' he replied.

'She won't give up until you're dead, Tom,' interrupted Edward.

'Thanks for that, Edward, but as we all know she's already had a go and failed. Maybe she'll realise now it's no good. She'll just give up and let me get on with my life.' Tom was rankled that Edward had interrupted Felix.

'Edward's right, Tom. She won't give up that easily. This is personal for her, and as we all know, her grip on reality is precarious right now to say the least. Who knows what's going on in that mind of hers, or what fur-brained scheme she will come up with next? No, we'll wait for her to make the next move, but we'll be ready for them,' said Felix, looking at Claudia and taking her paw in his. 'We're in this together.'

'I think you'll find Sophia and I still have a bit of unfinished business, Felix,' said Claudia. 'I haven't finished with her yet, or,' she added, 'she with me, I'm sure.'

Felix squeezed her paw affectionately. 'All in good time,' he said. 'Can't we just enjoy being in each other's company for a while, friends and family together?' He reached out and took Edward's paw too. Tom looked at Claudia and thought for a split second a wary look crossed her face – then it was gone. He told himself he was seeing things and turned his back on Felix and Edward to chat to Meissa, who was still seated by his side.

When they had all regaled each other with their tales of the battle, they set about helping Claudia sort out the house. Agatha had made a start in the upper rooms, but as they moved from room to room with brushes and pans in their paws, Tom realised this would take much longer than an afternoon's tidying to sort out.

'Claudia, I'm so sorry for all this mess,' he said to her, as they worked side by side in an upper drawing room.

'Why are you sorry? It's not your fault,' Claudia replied, still busy with a brush, sweeping up broken ornaments.

Tom sat back on his hind paws. 'It is my fault. If Zachariah hadn't brought me here then none of this would have happened. You would all be living normal lives and the Ce wouldn't have done this.'

'I'm sure this was all foretold in the stars, long before you showed up on my doorstep, Tom. You are meant to be here, with us, and let's face it, if circumstances had been different then I wouldn't have got to have a cat fight with Sophia this morning. And don't tell Felix, but I so enjoyed it. Next time, she won't get off so easily. No, you're one of us, Tom. You might be next in line to lead the Cait of Ce, but you're also half an Order of the Cataibh kitten too, don't forget that. It would always have come to this moment, maybe not now, but sometime.' Claudia put down her brush and gave him a hug. 'I think of you and Zachariah as my kittens, whether you're blood or not. Never forget that, and I will fight tooth and claw to defend you both, always.'

'Thank you, Claudia,' Tom managed to say, before his eyes welled with tears.

Meissa entered the room with a feather duster in her paw.

'Has anyone seen Edward?'

Claudia and Tom separated. He turned his head so Meissa wouldn't see him crying.

'Oh!' she said. 'I'm sorry. I'll go.' She turned to leave

the room, but Claudia called her back.

'Meissa, come here. I was just telling Tom that he is one of the family, as are you, be it by circumstance, blood, or marriage.' Claudia raised her eyebrow and looked at Tom when she said the word "marriage". He had the good grace to blush.

Meissa came over and sat on the arm of a chair beside Claudia.

'Thank you, Claudia, I appreciate that. Nobody can replace my parents, but it's good to know I'm not alone in the world,' she said, reaching out to Claudia. Claudia clasped her paw between her own.

'You are never alone. You will always have us,' she said.

Tom sat looking at these two very different and very important queens in his life. He felt so happy in that moment; then a thought crept into his mind.

'Where *is* Edward?' he said to no one in particular.

'I don't know, that's why I was asking you,' replied Meissa. 'The last time I saw him was when we were having lunch. I haven't seen him since. I'm sure of it.'

'Come to think of it, I haven't seen him since then either,' said Claudia. 'Maybe he's with Zachariah or Tarquair. I know Felix went into town to see about replacing some of the furniture. Maybe he went with him. Why did you want him?'

'No reason,' replied Meissa. 'I just thought it strange that I hadn't heard hide nor hair of him since, that's all.'

'I don't like him,' Tom said. 'I just don't trust him. I get this feeling.'

'He's Felix's brother, Tom, and if he trusts him, so should you,' said Claudia.

'How can you say that when he betrayed you?' Tom blurted out. 'How can you trust him?'

'I trust him because Felix trusts him. Now that's the end of the matter.' Claudia picked up her brush and walked out the room, leaving Meissa and Tom staring after her.

Meissa came over to him and put her paw on his.

'Claudia has known them both a lot longer than we have. You should trust her, Tom,' she said. She smiled at him, squeezed his paw then ruffled his fur on his head. He sighed and slumped his shoulders.

'I just can't trust him, Meissa. I can't explain it. I just, I don't know, I just sense something's not right about him.'

She leant over and kissed him on the cheek.

'Then follow your instinct, Tom. Go find him and sort it out. You won't be happy until you do.'

Tom looked at her, amazed that this feisty, strong-willed, awe-inspiring cat had just kissed him again.

'I'll still be here when you get back,' she said, 'and you might want to close your mouth. You'll catch flies!'

Tom stood up and took a few steps towards the door, then turned, ran back to Meissa and kissed her. He ran back out the room before she could say anything. Then he grabbed his jacket and headed out onto the street to find Edward De'Ath.

As soon as Tom was outside, he stopped. He took a deep lungful of the freezing cold air, which shocked his lungs into a fit of coughing. He felt like he had been holding his breath all day and the sudden breath of fresh, cold air was glorious.

Now, where would he find Edward? In truth he knew nothing about this cat other than he was Felix's brother, so he may as well start there. Mind made up, he headed towards Felix's house. He walked briskly through the streets towards a place that felt so familiar it was like his second home. There was a bounce in his step and a tune on his lips. He had kissed Meissa, he thought to himself. She had kissed him. They had kissed each other. The mere thought of it made him so happy he could have danced all the way along the street. He was skipping along the kerb, playing name games in his mind – Meissa Angel, Mrs Tom Angel, this is my wife Meissa – when a vaguely familiar cat stopped and asked him the time. Tom pulled out his fob watch to check it. The next thing he knew, he was plunged into darkness.

When he came to, his head was spinning, the world around him was dark, and his hind paws had been lifted from the ground and he was being hustled away by rough paws. Bumped and jostled along, he could tell he was being carried by several cats. His body was twisted this way and that as they struggled to walk in unison. He tried to yell out, but a muzzle had been put on his face so he couldn't make a noise. Every now and again there would be urgent whispers among his kidnappers, and he could feel himself being dragged down some stairs or back up them, he assumed to evade detection of passers-by. It didn't feel that too much time had passed before they paused, and Tom could hear the muffled sound of a door being thumped and then the sudden warmth as he was carried indoors. Once more he could hear muffled voices, and then another door being opened, and he was carried downstairs and into a room where he was dumped onto a hard stone floor with the covering still over his head. He struggled to wrestle himself free of the fabric and he felt paws grab at him, grapple his paws behind his back and truss him up like a chicken before leaving him there. Tom couldn't work out whether the room was dark or if it was just his covering, but after exhausting himself struggling to free himself from his ties, he fell asleep, only to wake up to the realisation that someone else was in the room with him. As he fought to get his bearings, he could hear someone moving around the room. Going by the sound of the footsteps, it was a smallish room, and his gaoler was mumbling. He couldn't make out what they were saying. They seemed to be having a conversation with someone, but Tom could only hear one person, and no one was replying. It was a queen's voice, quiet and childlike, as if she were talking to a parent. He could feel himself hold his breath again... It couldn't be. There was no way! But when he listened there was no mistaking the voice. What was Sophia still doing in Edinburgh?

Tom lay as still as he could, hardly daring to breath, trying to think through his options. As far as he could see it, he was lying in a room - where, he didn't know - tied up, unable to move, with a cat who, incidentally, was his mother, yet was desperate to kill him because she had some mad idea that he wanted to take over from her and her crazy cat clan. And he didn't have any way of defending himself. Great, he thought, I'm doomed! His heart started beating loudly in his head and he could almost sense the blood moving through his veins. That was it! He had to use his senses to fight Sophia. There was nothing else for it. Tom concentrated on his breathing, just as Felix had taught him, feeling the energy pulse down through his body, but he couldn't feel it. His mind kept wandering and focusing in on Sophia's mad mumblings. Who was she talking to? Think of the white energy flowing through my body, he thought to himself, still trying to make himself small so she wouldn't notice him. As he moved, he scraped something on the floor and he heard her footsteps stop. He held his breath waiting for her to resume. Tom heard her turn and walk to what felt like inches away from him. She started talking again to herself.

'You are my kittens, I love you so much,' she half-whispered. 'You'll be with me forever. No one can take you from me – you're mine.' He heard the pawsteps start to shuffle away and then she stopped and turned to him again.

'Felix doesn't love us anymore, my little babies. It's just us now. Felix doesn't love us. He never loved us, never wanted us, never wanted me...' Her voice trailed off into the softest whisper and Tom had to strain to hear it.

He felt sorry for her; she sounded so weak and vulnerable. Then he felt the first kick, then again and again. The kicks were coming hard and fast and Sophia was screaming at the same time as she landed each one of them. Tom was defenceless, trussed up like that, he couldn't even try to shield himself from the blows. As suddenly as it started, the kicking stopped, and Sophia stood panting. Tom could hear her every breath. Then she turned, walked quickly with her light little steps, and then he heard the door slam behind her.

Alone in the room again, Tom exhaled. He hadn't realised he had been holding his breath the entire time she had been here. Then, relieved that she had gone, he relaxed and started to sob. He lay there on the floor sobbing to himself, unable to even wipe the snot from his own nose. Tom cried for Sophia, and what must have happened to her to make her like this; and for Felix who had lost his beloved all those years ago; and for all those cats she had killed in the name of loyalty and power, but most of all he just cried for himself. For being alone in the world and unwanted by everyone, including his own mother; for feeling lost and lonely and not having anyone who knew how he felt. And he cried because for all of his short life he had held it in and tried to carry on no matter what happened to him, but he couldn't do that any longer; he couldn't hold onto the pain. He had to feel it to let it go. He lay there crying until the cloth round his face was wet with tears and snot, and he felt exhausted. He no longer had any tears left to cry and he felt every shooting pain through his body. He tried to concentrate on his energy, but he felt completely depleted. How on earth was he going to get out of here when he couldn't even summon up the energy to use his senses properly?

Tom lay there in the dark and thought about all

the cats he had loved in his life. He thought about brave Zachariah, throwing himself into the fray for him, no matter what, always the loyal friend; Meissa, the beautiful, feisty little firecracker who for some mad reason seemed to be in love with him; Claudia, gentle, caring Claudia, who gave shelter, food and love to an unwanted ginger kitten she didn't know and treated him as her own; and, of course, Felix. Strong, brave, loyal and gentle, Felix was everything Tom aspired to be – and more, he was Tom's father! He felt a rush of pride at these amazing cats who were all part of his life, and he could feel the stirrings of energy in the pit of his stomach. Even though it was dark, he closed his eyes and imagined himself back in the room with Felix, who was talking Tom through how to use his senses to help himself. He could feel the white heat of the energy building inside of him, and he could hear Felix's voice telling him to focus on the light, and feel the energy move through all his body until he could sense that his entire body was a pure golden light shimmering in the darkness. He focused on the M on his forehead, his third eye, and tried to view the room. At first everything was a dark sludgy grey, and he could hardly make out the floor in front of his face, but the more he concentrated, the brighter the room became. When he turned his head slowly around to look at the room he was held captive in, he got a horrible feeling in the pit of his stomach. Tom let out a gasp of incredulity. There was no way he could be here. How could Sophia be here? Inside the Order's headquarters. Inside Felix's house?!

The mosaic of fighting cats was beneath Tom's trussed body and the sconces on the wall were darkened. He tried to remember the way his kidnappers had taken him. Either they really didn't know Edinburgh, or they were trying to disorientate him. They must have doubled back on themselves at least twice before bringing him here. But what was the point in that, he thought to himself? Surely, they would have realised that as soon as he opened his eyes he would know where he was. Then the truth of the situation dawned on him. He hadn't opened his eyes! Even if he had, it was still pitch-black in here, so he would have no way of knowing where he was. Which meant that the Ce cats, and more importantly, Sophia, didn't know that Felix had taught him how to use his senses to see in the dark. He tried to remember if Felix had mentioned it in company, whether Flynn or Edward had been in the room at any time when he had tried to use it, but he didn't think they had. That gave him an advantage, but he still couldn't see how he could use it to his benefit. He could see whoever was in the room with him, but what use was that when he was still trussed up like a chicken and unable to move or call out? Then he remembered Felix showing him how to use his energy to bring items to him. Tom looked around the room slowly, using his senses, trying to see what he could use to cut the ties. Nothing. He sighed; he didn't know what to do next. It was a bloody stupid idea anyway.

Tom lay there getting progressively more dejected by the minute when he heard the door of the room open behind him. One of the Ce warriors came in and stood in front of him, looking down at him. He could see a knife glinting in his holster by his hip, but he couldn't figure out a way of getting it off him, even with the power of his mind. The Ce cat looked around, raised his arm, and all the sconces sprang into light. Of course, Tom was forgetting that it was dark, even though he could see. The Ce cat was carrying what looked like a small bowl, and once the room was lit, he gave Tom a quick kick in the legs and shoved the bowl down beside him.

'Eat,' he said, pulling the covering off Tom, then roughly unbuckling the muzzle from his face. He kicked Tom again, before turning and leaving the room. He was either very stupid or negligent in his duties, but Tom wasn't sure quite how he thought he could eat with his paws behind his back and no knife or fork. Then, Tom realised that the Ce thought Tom would have to eat like the animal they thought he was, with his mouth. Well, Tom thought to himself, he'd rather starve. He lay listening to his stomach rumbling at the smell of the food, watching the flames flicker on the walls, and then it suddenly dawned on him: he could use the gaslight in the sconces to burn through the ropes binding his arms and legs. Then he could escape, somehow. Tom managed to wriggle over to the wall and with great effort propped himself up against the wall. He tried to straighten up, but time and time again he was thwarted by the fact that the rope tightened each time. He was in the middle of trying to work out a way of jumping up to the sconce to hook himself onto it, when the door opened and Sophia walked in.

'So, you don't appreciate your mother's cooking, I see,' she said, prodding the bowl with the toe of her boot.

'I would rather starve than take something from you, and you're no mother of mine,' Tom said, trying to stand up as straight as he could, so he could look her in her eye.

'I do love a cat with principles,' she replied, coming over to him, so they were almost whisker to whisker. 'I've killed Felix. He squealed like a kitten as I did it. Begged me to make it quick, but I was having too much fun.'

The complacency with which she told him she had killed Felix took Tom's breath away. He couldn't be dead. Tom could feel the blood draining from his head, but he refused to cry.

'You're lying,' Tom said, looking her straight in the eye and hoping that she wouldn't realise he was half-pleading for the truth from her.

'Would I?' she replied. 'Would I lie to my own kitten?'

'He's not dead, I can feel it,' Tom said with more conviction than he felt.

Sophia touched Tom's face with her claw, drawing it slowly down from his ear to his mouth.

'Oh, don't worry, Tom. You'll be with him very soon because I'm going to kill you too.'

She pushed him on the side of his head with her paw and he wobbled and fell, hitting the floor hard with his cheek. She put her boot on the small of his back, leaned down and he felt a sharp pain.

If this is dying, it's not as bad as I imagined, Tom thought, as he felt warmth surging through his veins. He could sleep now, he thought.

'Don't just lie there. Get up, you stupid kitten!' Sophia was speaking to him, so he couldn't be dead, not yet.

Tom moved his paws cautiously and found that the ropes had been cut through. He moved his legs slowly, letting the blood flow back to them, so he didn't get a rush of blood.

'I said get up, you stupid ginger kitten!' Sophia aimed a blow at Tom's stomach but he caught her leg before it made contact with him.

'Now, now, Sophia,' Tom said, 'that's not playing

fair.' He twisted her leg, and she yowled in pain. 'And don't call me a stupid ginger kitten!'

'I'll call you what I like,' she said, trying not to show the pain on her face as he continued to twist her leg. 'You're mine.'

Tom pulled her leg away from her so she landed on the floor beside him.

'I will *never* be yours, Sophia!' His face was next to hers where she lay, and he could see the fear flicker in her amber eyes. The same eyes as his.

He pounced on top of her, his paw on her throat. She started to pant, the pressure on her windpipe increasing the longer his paw stayed there. With an almighty effort she managed to get her hind paws under his body and gave a tremendous push, knocking him off her and onto the floor. As she pounced on him, Tom scrambled to his paws, and she missed him, only catching his tail as she skidded past, hitting the wall behind him. Spun round by his tail, he was momentarily disorientated, and by the time he worked out where Sophia was, she was on her paws ready to dive at him again. He dived at her at the same time and they clashed in mid-air, claws and fur flying. They hit the floor as one cat, hissing and spitting, biting and clawing, for all they were worth. This was a battle for survival. They both knew that only one cat would come out of the room alive.

Sophia was on top of Tom biting into his scruff, rendering him useless, and he flailed his paws around until he caught her tail and twisted it. She yowled and leapt off him like he was on fire, but she backed off and started muttering to herself again. Tom got to his paws and stared at her in disbelief. What was going on? It was only then he realised that he was glowing again, very subtly shimmering, but in the dim gaslight he looked like he had been gilded in gold. Tom glanced down at his paws and claws, and he could see little sparks of light coming from the ends of them. It even scared him to see it, and it was his body. He felt strangely powerful and strong, even though he was terrified by what was happening to him. Sophia looked even more frightened than Tom felt.

'Devil!' she yelled at him, pointing at him as though they were in a crowd of cats. She started a low growling yowl deep in her throat.

It was terrifying to see her like this – she was like a little child. But she started yowling even louder. As he went to her, she flew at him once more, shrieking and thrashing her claws at him. Tom tried to cover his face and body, but her claws were slashing all over him. She was completely hysterical, and there was no way of stopping her. Her claws hit his face and sliced through his ear and eyebrow, and without thinking Tom lashed out, hitting her square in the face. She flew across the room, and hitting her head on a sconce, fell like a dead weight to the floor.

Minutes passed and neither of them moved. Tom could hardly breathe, he was so scared at what he had done. Slowly he tip-pawed over to her and nudged her with his boot; no movement. He knelt down beside her and put his paw on hers trying to feel a pulse. He started to panic. What was he going to do? Had he just killed the leader of one of the most feared cat tribes in the world? He couldn't think straight.

He heard the door open behind him, and Flynn and Felix partly fell through the door on top of each other. Felix went over to Tom and hunched down beside him.

Flynn ran to Sophia's side. He put his head into the fur at her neck and nuzzled her. Then very softly he began crying. At first there was no sound. Tom watched as tears rolled down Flynn's cheeks, wetting the fur on his face. Then a very small sound came from him – it sounded like he was humming at first – and Tom realised it was a much more primal sound, coming from Flynn's very soul. Tom felt hatred for himself, for having done this to Flynn's beloved Sophia, Tom's own mother.

Felix reached down to Tom's paw and removed it from Sophia's wrist where he was still holding her. Tom couldn't tear his eyes away from the sight of her, now lying in Flynn's arms. He was hugging her close, his head on her chest, breathing in her fur, and sobbing.

Felix put both his paws under Tom's arms and lifted him into his arms.

'How?' Tom whispered.

'Flynn came and got me from Claudia's,' replied Felix. 'Seems like Edward hasn't changed that much. He was entertaining his friends from the Cait of Ce here, in my home.'

Tom turned his head to look at Flynn cradling Sophia. 'What about them?'

'Flynn will be fine,' Felix said, and carried Tom out of the room.

TWENTY

Felix carried Tom out of the circular room and up the stairs. He brought him into the orangery where he laid him on one of the chaises. Ash appeared with a woollen rug to put over Tom and some hot water and bandages for his cuts. Tom closed his eyes and the tears flowed as he relived everything that had happened. It seemed so long ago that he and Zachariah had first sat in this room with Felix and he had told them of the Order of the Cataibh and the Cait of Ce. Life had been so different then. Tom had thought he was such a big cat, but in reality he was just a little kitten, fresh out of the orphanage. Felix dabbed at his scratches. Tom winced each time he touched them. The cuts were deep and kept flowing with blood, despite Felix's best efforts to stem them. Every time Tom shut his eyes he could see Sophia lying there, looking like she was sleeping, so peaceful. Then he remembered that she had been his mother, and the tears would start again. Tom heard in the distance a door bang twice and footsteps coming into the room, but he didn't open his eyes; he just felt too exhausted, completely and utterly drained, and just too tired to open his eyelids. A familiar voice brought him back to the present.

'They've gone. I don't know which way they went. Do you want me to find them?' Zachariah's voice seemed some distance away, but Tom could hear the concern in it anyway.

'No, leave them be. They should be allowed to mourn in peace,' Felix said, stroking Tom's fur.

The rhythmic motion lulled Tom to sleep, and he lost track of who was saying what. When he came to again, there was a different voice speaking, one he didn't recognise. As he opened his eyes in a long slow blink, he caught sight of the vet who had attended to Shepard's injuries. The vet was sitting by his side, carefully wrapping Tom's wounds in gauze and bandage.

'Felix?' Tom asked. The one word was all he could manage.

'He's close by, Tom,' the vet replied. 'He won't be leaving you, don't worry. Here, drink this. It will help with the pain and make you sleep.' He handed Tom a small glass with a brown liquid in it.

'I don't want to sleep,' Tom implored him. 'I don't want to have dreams about the fight.'

'It's fine. This will make sure you have a dreamless sleep. It will let you recover.' The vet nudged the small glass again and reluctantly Tom sipped from it. He remembered nothing else.

Tom woke to a bright day outside. He was back in his own room at Claudia's house, and he could tell by the tightness in his body and face that his scratches were beginning to heal. All was quiet in the house and he could hear it creaking and groaning the way old houses do. Tom lay back on the thick down pillows and closed his eyes again. He could feel himself start to purr. He was toasty warm, he was in his own bed and it was a beautiful day outside. Maybe it had all been a bad dream; maybe this was part of the dream. He leant out of the bed gingerly and pulled the bell cord. It wasn't Agatha who appeared a few moments later, as the door was flung open, but a ball of lilac fur, flying at him from across the room. For a moment Tom panicked, thinking Sophia had come back, but when she threw her paws round his neck and started covering him in kisses, he relaxed and laughed. Tom pulled Meissa away from him so he could see her beautiful face. Behind her, Zachariah, Claudia and Felix were coming into the room.

There were then many hugs and kisses from all around, including from Zachariah, who ribbed Tom by saying he was just glad that he was still alive, so Claudia could pick on Tom for a change instead of him. At one point Meissa and Claudia were both lying across Tom in his bed, hugging each other and crying. That is, until Felix pointed out that Tom was still trying to heal and unless they wanted him to break another rib or two then they had better move off him.

After they had all calmed down, Felix managed to persuade the queens to go downstairs and help Agatha prepare some food for the invalid. Zachariah wandered off to doze in his armchair by the fire, which finally left Tom and Felix by themselves.

'They're all very excited to see you awake at long last. You've been out cold since yesterday,' Felix said, perching on the side of the bed. 'I'm glad to see you awake.' He leant over and squeezed Tom's paw.

Tom asked the question that had been on his mind since the day before.

'What happened to Sophia?' he asked. It didn't seem right to call her his mother.

'Flynn took her away. I don't know where he took her—' Felix stopped; but Tom knew he had meant "her body".

'Why?'

'Why what?' said Felix, puzzled at his question.

'Why do this? Why do all of this just to kill me? I didn't mean to hurt her, Felix. I meant her no harm.' The tears started rolling down Tom's face again.

'I know, Tom, I know,' Felix said, rubbing Tom's paw.

'Why didn't she drown me like the other kittens? Then she wouldn't have put both of us through this.'

He was sobbing out loud as he struggled to speak. It was hard enough to come to terms with what he had done to Sophia without having the knowledge that she had tried to kill him as a kitten.

'It was Kasperi who saved you. He told Flynn to take you to the orphanage. Flynn suspected you were Sophia's kitten, but he didn't know you were mine. Sophia didn't know you were alive until Kasperi was dying. He kept you safe from her, but I suppose the grief caused by him dying, and finding out about you, tipped her over the edge.' Felix shrugged his shoulders. 'Who knows what went on in that mind of hers?'

'Why did he save me?'

'As the eleventh generation to rule the Cait of Ce, you would have become the most powerful cat in Scotland, the world perhaps. Eleven is a very powerful number to cats, he would have known that. He was a very wise cat. Kasperi knew who you were destined to become, maybe he could see the cat you would grow up to be. He was a good cat, your grandfather.' Felix leant over and kissed Tom on the forehead. 'You're very like him.'

'Felix, just one more thing. How did I manage to overpower Sophia? I'm just a skinny ginger kitten.'

Felix laughed. 'She forgot one notable thing about you, and that was, you aren't just some skinny ginger kitten. You're our kitten, Sophia's and mine. And together we made one hell of a smart, tough, fierce, intelligent, beautiful kitten. And that was her downfall, Tom. She underestimated you, and you should never do that with a De'Ath, especially my son.'

He hugged Tom close and Tom started to purr loudly as Claudia and Meissa came into the room laden down with trays of food, and Zachariah arrived, following his nose and his stomach.

EPILOGUE

The airship whirred and hummed as it made its way back to the broch. Sophia lay outstretched on a bed. The Ce warriors sat at the other end of the gondola, avoiding looking at their fallen leader. Flynn paced back and forth like a caged lion. The warrior's medic was beside Sophia. He pulled her cloak further up her body to cover her, before standing and approaching Flynn. Flynn grabbed him by the shoulders and pulled him close, so the cat's face was level with his. The cat swallowed hard then nodded his head once.

'She lives.'